# SANCTUARY WITHIN THE BREED

## LUCIFER'S BREED MC
## BOOK 1

### BY RYDER DANE

ISBN-10# 1-945012-14-5

ISBN-13# 978-1-945012-14-3

Artwork by Jess Buffett Graphic Designs

Published by Vinvatar Publishing
Website: Vinvatar.com

# TABLE OF CONTENTS

# CHAPTER ONE

Baron watched as the boys blew off some steam in the isolated diner. The women were fair game and had stopped pretending to be outraged an hour ago. Homer, Barney, and Zippy were working their skinny asses off trying to out fuck each other while they shared the chunky waitress named Fran. She was an older woman with pretty, dark, curly hair that was being pulled backwards as Homer pulled her ass back over his prick. Zippy was lying on the padded bench they'd pulled out of the booth, and Fran's snatch had him buried inside her puffy lips. Barney was having a few desperate last strokes through her wide lipstick smeared lips, and one by one the guys yelled out their orgasms. The boys lost points on that fuck. Fran didn't come.

He watched as Fran sat up and wiped the come from her chin. Homer let go of her hair and sat back on his naked ass on the linoleum, catching his breath. Zippy tried to push her off his hips and she slugged him on the jaw. "You broke dick motherfuckers can take your limp dicks out of here." She balanced her weight on her toes and pulled one thigh over Zippy to stand next to the bench. "Big Bad fucking bikers, get your asses gone before I call a cop. I should have known what you slick dicked bastards were when I let you talk me into this." She pulled her dress together and began buttoning it up as her mouth kept running, berating the men who gave their best, and it wasn't enough to make her happy.

Roley came up behind Fran and smacked her on the ass hard, and told her to "Bend over the table, bitch, you're gonna get what you want." He wasted no time slamming his dick into her cunt. He didn't spare the smacks on her ass and thighs while he swiveled his hips, reaming her sopping wet hole. "Grab them titties and squeeze the nipples, pull them out to the side so I can see that you're pinching them hard enough, hurry up, I ain't got all fuckin' day to play with you."

She looked back at him ready to tell him off, but the increased power behind his slaps on her ass seemed to do the trick and cause her to rethink because she let go of the table edge and crossed her arms to pinch her nips. He leaned over her and talked close to her ear, "Back that ass up on my dick, you dirty whore. You need fucked hard 'til you scream, dontcha, and I'm just the fucker to give you what you want. That's right, shove your big ass up, try to buck me off." He kept smacking her already red ass cheeks as she was screaming at him to fuck her.

"Fuck you, you're all a bunch of pussy boys with little dicks," had Roley laughing, his prick was a respectable eight inches, and he decided to give the horny waitress something to scream about. He pulled his prick from her cunt and lined it up at her asshole. "Yeah, since my cock isn't big enough for your sloppy cunt, you won't mind if I ream your asshole now, will you, bitch?" He didn't give her any other notice than that before he speared her hole and kept sliding inside while she screamed at him to take it out. Her words may have been believable if she hadn't begun humping her hips out for deeper penetration. "Reach down there and play with that clit of yours now, I'm getting ready to come and I want to feel your tight ass clamp down on my prick. Come on now, Yeah, that's better." Her fingers must have done the trick, because she shoved her ass up to meet his prick and screamed her pleasure out loud, just before he shouted and jerked his hips as he pumped his jizz in her back hole.

Baron wanted to laugh when Fran finally stood upright and turned into Roley's arms for a deep kiss.

Burger was sitting on one of the thick wooden chairs eating a hamburger while the waitress was eating him. The guy had the manners of a goat, proved by the way he kept telling her how he liked what she was doing, and the food was falling from his mouth while he talked. Skids hoisted her ass up so she stood on her feet still bent over Burger. He kicked her legs apart and pulled her little striped skirt up around her waist. The woman wasn't wearing panties, and Skids slapped that ass a few times as he dabbed his dick in the wet pool of juice slathered at her cunt. "Here you go, baby, you just keep sucking that fat sausage, and I'll fill this end." He slid his prick in, and immediately began to pump his hips to pave his way for deeper thrusts. The smacks on her ass seemed to inspire her to join in by moving her hips in time with his thrusts. She must be happier than Fran, because her hip action started to become erratic until Skids slapped her ass hard enough to gain her attention. "Slow the fuck down, wait 'til I tell you to come, bitch.

Burger enjoyed the sight of her red ass so much he shot his load in her mouth and patted her on the head. The man wasn't much on conversation, but he put himself away and left her a three dollar tip on the table. Skids did his trademark side to side move in her cunt and growled at her to "come if you plan to come at all." He let her ride her climax out on his softening cock. When he finally pulled away, he leaned over and kissed her red cheek. "Don't ever say I didn't kiss your ass."

Baron had seen the scene played out in many, many bars, diners, and small towns. If he hadn't gotten a blowjob from the twins this morning, he might be riding shotgun with one of the groups that were fucking the four women.

They had escorted Wolfman home after the meeting with the Burning Bastards MC. After the evidence and the drama that went with executing two of their own, and exiling another man, he was glad to be heading back to the crib. This diner was known to be "user friendly" and he was glad they'd stopped to grab some eats. It was a damn shame they didn't sell beer here, but there would be plenty for them at home.

He headed for the door, someone had to get these boys on the road, so it might as well be him. He left enough money on the register to pay for the gas and food, even though many groups would consider that stupid. He was too close to home to want to hurt the small businesses that tolerated the Breed. The boys couldn't have unwound like this in a chain restaurant, the heat would have been all over them within minutes.

Other than seeing vehicles pull over to allow the small horde of bikes to pass, the rest of the ride was uneventful. They'd been gone for less than four days, but Wolfman and his entourage had been guests of the chapter for a week before and during the talks. Wolfman was the National President of Lucifer's Breed MC. They had ten chapters and were a presence in the southwestern states. Some called them one percenters, but they were more civilized than that. At least on the surface. They still raised a little hell, and not all of their activities to raise funds were straight up, but they didn't chase old ladies down on their bikes to steal their purses either.

Gunner, Preacher, and Leech, were at the club when they pulled in. Some of the group had peeled away to go to their homes in the area, on the last leg of their trip. Some headed directly for the bunkhouses and the rest found the bar for an icy one to wet their dry throats.

Baron yanked a chair from under the table and turned it around to use the back as an armrest. "So according to Wolfman, Reeker has been recruiting the Prospects from the Bastards and we have no doubt he has been grooming a few of ours too. We need to know which ones are drifting into the no return, and any other information about them. They stole a few rat bikes from the Bastards and from what their Prez says, they will live long enough to regret it, if riding bikes with no brakes and fucked up bald assed tires are any measure. He told Wolf that two of their Prospects have gone to the new group, not sure what they are calling themselves, but from the description of the patch, they are head cases to begin with. White background, magic marker drawing of a carbine crossed with a sword, and medieval weapons in the rim of the circle." He drank half of his beer, before continuing his update to keep the men informed.

Leech nodded his head, "From what I heard of the conversation, Wolf said to deal with it if it comes our way. Any action will be sanctioned."

Baron continued saying his piece, "He's dealing with some problems up north. I wish he hadn't allowed a club up there, that place has some crazy motherfuckers with doomsday theories and livin' the lifestyle of separation. They'd give those good old boy Swamp Rats clubs a go for the money, and I'm no pussy when it comes to weapons, but I've seen arsenals in desert bunkers that were not as full of explosives as these guys keep around."

Mortimer Leech, aka The Leech, was the kind of man that never met a stranger, and could ferret out information in the blink of an eye. He was looking all smug and shit when Baron looked his way. Gunner spoke up and grinned to his companions, "Guess who finally got Ms. Hightits to break down and give him a blowjob? He had to give her a good tongue lashing first, but I have to tell you, I am jealous. The bitch has skills. She kept asking when you would be back, and I kept telling her what you said about visiting one of your fuck me girls in Kansas. Pissed her off, and Leech here caught her in a moment of weakness."

"Son-of-a-bitch. You did it?" At Leech's grin and nod, Baron reached into his front pocket and pulled out a roll of cash. He flipped a hundred to Leech and added another fifty. "Thanks, I couldn't get her to let my dick go long enough to take a piss. Now that she's fucked with another guy, I can get away from her. I still think she wanted to lock my ass down into an eighteen-year sentence. She has that predatory look about her. You know the look they give you when females are picking out a new old man and he isn't biting the hook."

Preacher was nursing his beer, he was a brooding fucker, but a good man to have around, and on the occasional need for a burial, he could out preach any Southern Baptist preacher. He was well built, at least the ladies thought so, and his motto was "an eye for an eye". No slight was allowed to go by when it came to the invisible lines he drew and others occasionally crossed. Unlike his religious peers, he was a firm believer in birth control, divorce, and encouraging people to get by as best they could. He smoked a bit of weed, and could curse with the best of them, yet hearing the word Goddamn, would put him in a killing mood. "Perhaps I should give another sermon at Church tonight? I believe the last one wasn't taken seriously."

His last sermon resulted in baskets filled with condoms set out on the bar. There were a few men who refused to use them, and if a woman didn't have her birth control on board, they were playing with pregnancy. Preacher was an odd duck, but he was a good man to have at your back, and afterwards, he would pray your sins away for you.

Baron needed to go home to his own place. Melvin was being taken care of by Gunner, but the little shit ass tended to go off his feed when Baron wasn't there for more than a day. Melvin was a short-legged black and brown, shaggy little dog that showed up at his house one day and never left. That was three years ago. The little fucker had an interspecies thing going on with one of the barn cats, and until he saw it with his own eyes, he wouldn't have believed a mangy yellow tomcat would allow a short shaggy Melvin to pin him down and hump him, but he did.

He hated to sit his ass back in the saddle after so many hours riding today, but it was his transportation home and it was only a twenty-minute ride to his place, so he sucked up the stiffness and drove the distance. He was proud of his home, it wasn't fancy, but it worked for him. His home was a large, four bedroom log cabin situated in the center of twenty-two acres of hardwoods. His pole barn had more than enough projects to keep him busy for the rest of his life, if he planned it out right. Melvin greeted him a hundred feet from the door.

Baron had to stop the bike and hoist the short critter up in front of him to ride the rest of the way home. Melvin loved to sit his ass back on Baron's seat between his thighs, and prop his front paws on the gas tank for his victory ride into the lean-to, next to the house where the bike was parked when he was at home.

He pulled his saddlebags off the rear fender, and Melvin trotted into the house through his dog door, while he had to use the key. "There's something not right about this," he told the brown-eyed pooch. "You come and go at will and I own the place but need to use a damn key." Melvin wasn't impressed.

He popped a cardboard frozen pizza in the toaster oven and set the dial while he stripped off his clothes in the mudroom. The extra change of jeans and four t-shirts joined the clothes in the washer, and he made a mental note to turn it on when he got out of the shower. He walked into the bathroom and looked at the scruffy looking bum in the mirror. He needed a haircut and a shave too. And since he was the kind of man that would bathe in a cold ass river rather than go feeling filthy, he took the time to shave once the shower had rinsed four hundred miles of road dirt from his body. He left the moustache, dark goatee, and the thin line of dark whiskers along his jawline, because he liked it.

He dabbed some cream on his pierced nipple, where his cut had rubbed the tip raw after a rain cloud decided to follow them for a fifteen-minute shower. Maybe he should have the soft leather vest lined with something so it wouldn't rub like that.

He walked naked into his bedroom, and thought about Ms. Hightits, as she was affectionately called by most of the men at the club. She had been a good lay, and Gunner was right, the woman had skills that a man could appreciate. The problem was, he wasn't ready to lock down with any woman yet. Not to mention, he wasn't thrilled with the idea that over half of the club had already enjoyed her charms. He wasn't going to look for a virgin when he finally invited a woman to be his old lady, but drug addicted and/or alcoholic discarded toys weren't his idea of what he wanted for the mother of his kid either.

Him and Gunner hadn't even decided if they wanted one woman so they could enjoy a good threesome relationship, or if they wanted to peel away from the ménage lifestyle altogether. He figured it would depend on the woman involved. They had been sharing women for years, and it would be tough to change their favorite sexual practice. Neither man wanted to fuck the other, but feeling another man's cock rubbing along his with only a thin rubbery membrane between them was fucking amazing. Watching Gunner and their chosen bitch for the night going at it was like watching an interactive porno. He loved it. His friend liked to issue instructions while he watched him and the woman. Gunner was a bit on the dominant side.

Being honest with himself, yeah, he was as dominant as Gunner, and they were both more than a bit sadistic sexually. It had been a few months since they let Caroline leave them. She took whatever they dished out, but they knew she was only there for the pain and sex. When she began to fight with them to get them to beat on her, they refused. That wasn't ever going to happen. Finding out that she'd started cutting, they were done. She was now one of the whores in Wolfman's entourage. She got the kind of pain that he and Gunner would not give her. That was the end of that. It was also the last time they'd allowed themselves to enjoy a ménage together.

13

Maybe sometime in the future they would find another partner, but for now, they took care of their needs in the more conventional ways. Thinking about sex right now wasn't a good idea, but he took himself in hand, flipped a porno on the laptop, and took care of business. Melvin went into the kitchen to eat and drink, giving him the privacy he needed.

Baron slept until ten a.m. That was kind of late for him, but Melvin started wiggling around on the bed and farting near his face. The little bastard wanted him to unlock the dog door so he could go out and take his morning shit. He hurried to the door and opened it for the fur ball, then headed into the bathroom to deal with his own needs. There was a lot to do today, and he needed to get his ass in gear.

He called Gunner and they arranged to meet in the club's office to go over a few things that needed to be brought up tonight at Church. He also had a bag of income that had been dropped off in his absence that needed to be taken care of. He would feel a lot better when that particular chore was taken care of.

Melvin decided he wanted to go for a ride today, so Baron put the miniature cut the club's Bitches had made on him and small goggles to keep flying bugs from shooting into his eyes as they drove down the roads. With his studded collar and colors, declaring him one of the group, he looked bad assed and Baron told him so before they got on the bike. He could swear the little shit ass smiled as he sat back and planted his paws for balance.

# CHAPTER TWO

Amy Selters was ready to kill someone. Her little brother, David, was out of control. He had decided last year to try his hand at being a motorcycle bum, and she'd not seen him again until three days ago, when he broke into her apartment and demanded money. He looked nothing like the young man that left her care so many months ago. Now he was scruffy and from the sight of his bloodshot eyes, she would bet he was addicted to drugs too. He was so thin she would have been frightened for him, if he hadn't attempted to sell her for sex to his friends. He was a motorcycle bum all right, one of the worst cases of a thrown away life that she'd seen. Since she helped at the local soup kitchen, she'd seen plenty of kids just like David.

She'd refused to give him money, but had fixed him a bowl of soup and two thick sandwiches. She went to the bathroom and came back to see him letting two other men inside of her apartment. One was an older man who wore a full beard and hair to his shoulders. The other was another skinny man with a serious case of acne and the thinnest excuse for a moustache she'd seen. David was yelling at her for refusing to share her money with him. The older man they called Reeker, kept looking at her and finally told David, "Maybe we can work something else out, your sister seems to be the kind of woman that would be worth a hit or two. I'll give you a rock to keep you happy while I try her out, I know some people who might pay to fuck her, if she's any good. Hell, Stevie here can help me so we have two opinions."

That did it for her, she'd heard enough, seen enough and was done. She walked over to the open balcony sliding doors where David had broken into. She stepped through the ripped screen and started screaming her head off. "Help, someone call the police, help," and she screamed such a high pitch that she felt her ears pop. Since the balcony faced the pool area, most working people were home at this time of night, several people began running and yelling at her to stay where they could see her. Three of the men who lived there were prison guards in the next county. They were young and fit, they also carried guns when they left the prison for personal protection. She didn't see them running, darn it.

When the crowd of people raced up the steps to her apartment, the three men cursed her and ran down the steps through the crowd coming up the stairs. It caused a few to stumble and allowed them to escape. Her purse, with her car keys and bankcard, along with all of her personal information was gone with the men.

The police were acting as if she'd invited her brother inside, until she showed them the ripped screen door and pried latch, they finally began to take her seriously. Oscar Lime was the officer that talked to her, the tag on his shirt pocket called him the Chief of Police, and she was becoming more alarmed with every word coming out of his mouth. She was happy her social security card wasn't in her purse, because that and her birth certificate would have yielded the thieves even more money than just her bankcard and wallet with less than fifty dollars in it. They would probably sell the license and the rest of the stuff in her purse. She called and canceled her card, hopefully they hadn't used it yet. And the police report would help her with gaining new identification. She was advised to move to another location as soon as she could to keep David and his friends from finding her and trying again. In the meantime, she should get better locks and be careful when she was alone.

Oscar Lime, the Police Chief, was also where she heard about the 'wanna' be' bike gang trying to establish themselves in the area. She was so pissed by the time he finished telling her about David's defection from the bikers that he was prospecting for, that she wished she had the president of Lucifer's Breed in her hands, she almost ached to bust him with a baseball bat. She often saw the overgrown juvenile delinquents riding through town like they owned the place.

It was a shock to her when she found out that several of them did in fact own many of the businesses in town. She walked past Cupid's Boutique and Classy B's Beauty Salon every morning on her way to work. She took her elderly 1971 Dodge Swinger that she'd inherited from her paternal grandmother, to a place called Gunner's. They were the only ones that knew how to fix the old crate, but she felt fortunate that someone knew about older model cars, and where to find parts to fix them.

Cowboy's Steakhouse and Grill was the best place in the whole county to get a delicious meal. Even the medical walk-in clinic was owned and run by members of the motorcycle club.

In the two and a half years she'd been here, she found out just how much the economy of Juanita, Missouri depended on the MC community. Being a dog groomer didn't put her into contact with many of the citizens of the area, but people did like to talk and gossip when they picked up their animals. She knew some of the members' wives or live-ins, because they brought their dogs in to be bathed or groomed. Furfur brought her two huge poodle mixed female dogs in every few weeks to get them bathed and groomed. The dogs were the size of Great Danes, and since the standard poodle mother had been the size of a small Shepard, it stood to reason the puppies would be huge too. Myrtle brought Melvin in for his monthly shampoo and manicure, and a smallish woman called Liberty brought in a grumpy Pit Bull named Jerome. The women never mentioned the MC Club, or anything about them. They spoke about the weather, the dogs, or a shoe sale.

She'd learned more about the people in the town than she wanted to know, but at least she now knew who the gossips were talking about when they couldn't resist making comments and judgments about others. Until her brother had joined her here, from his stint in Juvenile Detention for being incorrigible and malicious destruction of property just over a year ago, she had thrived and loved the town.

David was pretty much forced on her when their mother remarried for the fourth time, to a judge in their hometown of Norse, Missouri. Her mother had begged and heaped guilt on her shoulders until she'd consented to take him in. The understanding was that he would stay with her until he found a job and could fend for himself. The last day he'd spent at the apartment, he left a note, emptied out her wallet, and tried to hotwire her car. She called her mother, who was out of the house for the day, and got her new stepfather on the phone. He could tell that she was upset, and they talked for over an hour. He was a decent sort of man, practical and intuitive enough to know that she'd had it with her half-brother.

His best advice was, change the locks, and let the boy go. "Don't allow him to make you feel guilty and manipulate you into giving him money or a place to stay. He's burned his bridges, and frankly, Amelia, I am surprised he lasted as long as he did, before showing his true colors. No one owes him anything, and he needs to understand that. I have met him, and I was not impressed in the least with his cocky attitude and childish actions. The boy also had a drug problem before he went to detention, I don't imagine your mother told you about that, did she?"

Amy had to admit she knew next to nothing about David. "I barely knew him before he moved in with me. All I ever heard was that he was headstrong and had some problems at school."

"Do you mean to tell me that you didn't know David's father was a biker? Don't get me wrong here, my brother is a Sergeant-at-Arms with a group out of Ohio. He is also one of the lawyers for the club. I have very little connection with him due to my job as a judge, however, I love him and respect his life choices. My point is, we can hope your brother falls in with a group that values intelligence and has rules to follow or consequences to face if those rules are not followed. They might turn him into a man that you can feel respect for. Give it a chance, but refuse to allow him to manipulate you. That is my best advice."

She had listened to Thomas's advice over the past year, and only gave her brother money at Christmas and on his birthday. She bought gift cards at fast food places so he could get a burger and fries if he was hungry. Twice he'd come to her place drunk and demanding money, and now he'd gone as far as she would allow him to go. She would be signing the complaint with the Sheriff's department in the morning, and they would prosecute him, if what Oscar said was true. Maybe if he was forced to spend time in jail, it would save his life.

After a restless night's sleep where she'd dreamt of David in a coffin and David being beaten up, and even of the older man, Reeker, that was a frightening dream. In her dream, he came into her room and twisted her arms behind her while ordering her brother to use his fists on her to get her to tell them the pin number for the bankcard they'd stolen. Thankfully she had woken and the dream faded, but not her determination to give the men in charge of the Lucifer's Breed a piece of her mind.

They were partially responsible for David's newest lowlife activity, and she planned to tell them so.

She went to the Sheriff's department first, to sign whatever papers they needed to prosecute the three men. By eleven o'clock she was waiting at the gate for permission to enter the grounds of the motorcycle club's sanctuary. The young men at the gate seemed more interested in her car than in her. She didn't know if she should be flattered or insulted by the way one of the men kept petting the shiny green fender, and saying things like "sweet ride, and classic beauty" as the men talked while they waited.

The go-ahead must have been given, and they waved her through. She parked the car in front of the cement block building and locked it up before walking to the entrance. She didn't know what the protocol was for entering a place like this. Was she supposed to knock? Did they have a secret password? Her problem was solved when an older biker, with a black skullcap and chaps, walked past her and held open the door for her to enter the building before him.

She thanked him and he nodded his head before heading to the door at the back of the room with a picture of a male stick figure taking a leak. She looked around the room and saw a woman behind the bar with a phone to her ear while she laughed hard, so hard she appeared to be choking. Amy headed to the bar.

She perched on a stool, and waited for the woman to acknowledge her presence. She had no idea she was facing the camera that was hidden behind the stuffed rat collection on the shelf below a picture of old Hollywood's 'Rat Pack' of Sinatra, Martin, Bishop, Davis, and Jones.

The woman with the phone stuck to her ear was moving toward her, continuing her conversation with the person on the other end of the line. "I don't give a fuck what you say, I am not cleaning that up again, from now on, you take a shit, clean the bowl, don't leave it for someone else to have to see." She got to where Amy sat and rolled her eyes heavenward in impatience. She held up a finger for Amy in a wait a minute gesture, and finished her conversation. "I told you, I'm not your fuckin' maid, I want your ass out of my place today, pack your shit, and get out. I won't live like a damn pig, and I am too damn old to start now." She tapped the phone to hang up the line while a man's angry voice could be heard in the background.

"Fuckin' men, they move in with you and within a week, its do this, clean that, screw that shit. I can buy a fucking vibrating rubber dick to take his place for all the good he does me." She slapped a napkin down on the bar that looked like a salvaged bowling alley lane. "What can I get you to drink, Amelia Selters?"

Gunner, Baron, Cash, and Chaucer watched the TV screen on the wall of the office. They wondered what the pretty blonde with the curly hair falling down her shoulders wanted with 'The Bosses' of the club. She'd given her name to the Prospects at the gate, and told them who she wanted to talk to, but not about what.

She didn't fidget as most visitors to the club did. She perched on the barstool and seemed to be getting on like an old friend with Myrtle. No one got along with Myrtle for more than ten minutes before the cranky bitch eventually found their buttons to push that she exploited for her own amusement. The other female bartender was taking time to dry out, Geraldine was a nice lady with a bad drinking problem. She'd been forced to go into rehab for her alcoholism, or be pushed out of the club. Amelia Selters had already scored points for sticking around for almost half an hour.

Gunner leaned forward and cocked his head to the side. "I think I've seen her somewhere before. I just can't remember where." He liked what he saw, and provided she wasn't some kind of bubble-brained woman here to serve papers on them, he might give her some of his time.

Melvin woke from his nap and jumped onto Baron's lap. The dog caught sight of the woman on the screen and began to wiggle and whine. He jumped down and headed for the door, and Cash let him out. "What the hell? That little prick tried to bite me every time he saw me for the first six months that you brought him in the club. Now look at him." They all watched Melvin run as fast as his little legs would carry him toward the newcomer. He sat at the woman's feet and barked. They watched her jump a little and look down at the dog. Then watched her welcoming smile and the way she greeted Melvin, letting the little guy jump all over her once she got off the barstool.

Gunner laughed, and Baron quirked his lips. Melvin knew her that was for certain.

Myrtle and Amy laughed at Melvin's antics, and Amy showed the older woman what new trick he'd learned three days ago when he came in for his monthly grooming. She held up one hand and then the other, each time she held up her hand, his opposite paw would come up and high five it. "You can't go really quickly with him doing this, but he seems to like it." She put him through his routine of tricks and asked Myrtle if she had a treat for him for being such a good boy. Myrtle handed over a short stick of beef jerky the greedy fur ball snatched from Amy's fingers and ran off to hide under one of the tables in the room to enjoy.

Baron watched the woman ruffle the dog's fur, and all he did was hang his tongue out from the side of his mouth. The first time he'd tried that, Melvin had attempted to take off his fingers. The traitorous little dog was going to hear about this later. He shook his head watching Melvin roll onto his back and drop to his knees, hang his head and collapse in a heap, playing dead. Cash and Chaucer left the room to meet the woman and bring her back to join them.

Gunner was still grinning when Baron turned the screen off with the remote. "I like seeing that little fucker actually acting like a dog for once. He did everything she wanted him to do and if she looks as good up close and personal as she does on the screen, I might be willing to have her teach me a few tricks. You game?"

The door opened before he could reply, but once she'd entered the room, he looked over to his friend and nodded his head. "I'm game."

She was ushered into the room and waved into one of the chairs in a circle with Mel following right behind her. The one named Cash introduced each man in the room, and sat down in a chair near her. Baron, the club's President, was impressive to look at and Gunner, the VP, was just as eye catching. However now wasn't the time for her to get wet panties. The men called Cash and Chaucer weren't nearly as appealing, but they would give a girl reason to pause and sigh over.

Baron was a huge man with shaggy brown hair and eyes that looked like a sapphire in the sun. His nose had a small bump in it and he wore a well-trimmed goatee with a thin line of whiskers lining his jaw. His moustache was even trimmed at the lip line, and Amy liked the looks of the pierced ear with the thick gold hoop. With the rest of him, the earring gave him a pirate look, and she wished he wasn't one of the bikers.

Gunner had a harder look about him, he wasn't quite as tall as Baron. His hair was more red than brown, but not a true ginger. Still the hair was thick and could use a good stylist to tame the messy windblown look. He was sporting a scruffy crop of what appeared to be week old whiskers, and his full lips teased her to look and wonder how they would feel and taste. He had the darkest brown eyes, and they returned her interested look until she felt herself blushing.

She was having a hard time deciding which of the other two men was more attractive. Cash, who was a clean shaven, blue eyed charming devil, or Chaucer, that had eyes the color of tarnished brass, they changed with the light in the room and the tilt of his head to a silvery grey. He was built like she imagined a Viking as old romance novels described, except he was taller and broader. When he'd smiled, she couldn't help but notice the gold eyeteeth.

Every man in the room wore bold tribal tattoos and each had a dragon or some kind of mythical looking beast running from their elbows to up into their neckline. She would really like to see these men without shirts, but it wasn't the time to be fantasizing about gorgeous male bodies, even if she wanted to help them out of their clothes…while on her knees, with her teeth. The thought made her smile, but seeing their speculative looks, she sobered her own facial features.

"Thank you for seeing me, I am, as you know, Amelia Selters, my brother's name is David Gregory, and until last night, I thought he was a pledge to your motorcycle group. I know he was involved with your people because I dropped him off twice at the gate last fall. So please don't give me the know nothing about him excuse for allowing him to turn into the horrible creature that he has become. I have it on good authority that groups such as yours police their prospective members extensively and yet I see the drug addled creature that tried to sell his own sister for a fix to an equally drug fogged man named Reeker. They had another young man with them that had the most pitiful facial hair named Stevie.

"Last evening, David broke into my apartment and asked me for money. I refused to give it to him and he looked so pitifully skinny that I gave him a bowl of soup and a couple of sandwiches. I went to the other room and when I came back, he was letting the other two into my home. Words were said, and the man, Reeker, said he would give David drugs, if he and Stevie could try me out before selling me to other men. I managed to escape to the balcony and call for help, but they got away in the crowd coming to help me."

She sat back in the chair as poised as a young girl in church, and Baron was digesting her story when Gunner asked her what she expected from them.

"Expect? I would think it would be obvious. I want you to take care of your responsibility for him. He was clean when he came to your group. After all, he was only out of detention for a few weeks. He bragged to me about this place and how great the club was. He got back on drugs under your watch, and I expect you to fix this screw up on the part of the club."

Baron had heard enough. This pretty little woman wanted them to parent her brother? If she weren't so earnest, and if he didn't want to fuck her, he would have laughed and sent her out the way she came in.

# CHAPTER THREE

Gunner had no filter when it came to stupidity. He laughed out loud. "You expect us to parent your snot-nosed, drug addict brother? Lady, I don't know what you think about the Breed, but we only take on men who want to be here, and your brother snuck out of here like a goddamned little pissant in the middle of the night to follow Reeker. It was just as well that he left on his own, since he was about to be thrown out. And I do mean thrown. He was lazy, and had an ego problem that would have gotten him hurt in a physical way if he'd been here the morning after he allowed two underage girls in the club after dark.

"That little fucker endangered everyone here. If Myrtle hadn't seen the girls come in before someone grabbed them, contributing to a minor would be the least of our worries. Those little girls got the shit scared out of them and Myrtle and one of the other women took them home before anything bad happened to cause irreparable damage to them or the club. If their parents reactions were anything to go by, their twitchy tender asses are probably still grounded."

He was already out of his chair and leaning over hers with his hands on the arms of the chair she occupied. She fought the need to shrink back as far as possible. If she let him see how badly he intimidated her with words, she would never get them to help her find David and force him into rehab. She had to keep reminding herself to act like a lady. *You walk the walk and talk the talk, and you will be treated in the way you present yourself.* That is what her grandmother told her, and so far, the woman had been spot on. She kept her eyes trained on the knee of Baron's denim clad leg. Direct eye contact would be considered a challenge in any animal's behavior pattern, and these men were animals. She could feel her inner slut begging to invite him into even more aggressive behavior. She took a slow deep breath and stifled the bitch.

Melvin had been at her feet during the power play between her and Gunner. The little dog jumped up onto her lap while the big man loomed over her, and faced Gunner with teeth bared. The man ignored him, and Melvin began to growl a low threatening sound from deep down somewhere in his stiff little body.

"You want us to chase your coffin bait and spank him, you'd better be willing to give something in return." His demands were cut off by the evil Melvin, who'd stopped warning him and jumped at his face, ready to redecorate his features. Gunner barely got his arm up in time to avoid a direct bite to the mouth and nose. Instead, the ten pound fur ball latched his sharp teeth onto his forearm and was hanging on with every bit of his strength.

Gunner pulled back and stood with Melvin hanging on his arm. He turned away and tried to shake the canine loose, but that only caused the wounds to become more painful. "Lady, call this little fucker off or I will kill the son-of-a-bitch." He looked at Amy, but she was staring at the dog with her mouth open in shock. He turned to Baron, and spoke through gritted teeth. "Get him off, man, his teeth are like goddamn nails."

Baron tried to keep the smile from forming on his lips. Seeing his little buddy attack his best friend in defense of a woman like that was giving him a proud parent moment, but he could imagine how sharp those teeth were. It was still odd to him that Mel had attached himself to her so quickly. He reached out and grabbed Mel around his rib cage, and told him to let go. "Come on, buddy, you know Gunner wouldn't really hurt her. Let him go, man, he isn't near her." Nothing he said made a difference, until the troublemaker stepped into the dog's sight.

She held out her hands and lifted Mel up a few inches, "His teeth are stuck, he can't let go until the pressure is off of them." She stepped closer and hugged her rescuer, telling him what a brave little man he was. "It's alright now, Melvin, the mean man won't try to hurt me again. You are such a brave boy. Come on, you can let go now." The dog opened his jaws and Gunner was free. When she held him closer and bent her head over the mutt, and told him that his next grooming would involve a nice extra-long brushing for being such a great protector, Baron lost it completely. His laughter joined with Chaucer's and Cash's, as Gunner started yelling obscenities. He sat down, staring at the dog and woman as she made it sound like Melvin had single handedly saved her from a fate worse than death. It also explained why his dog was so attached to her. She must be the woman that gave him a bath and cut his nails each month.

Amy and Melvin slipped out of the room while three men were laughing and trying to help stem the blood trickling from the puncture wounds on Gunner's arm. She almost ran to the bar where Myrtle was, and handed the dog over to the older woman with a kiss to the top of his head. "Hide him, he bit Gunner," before she waved and ran out of the front door.

She was half afraid the men would call to the gate and refuse to allow her to leave, but they waved her through, so she left, wishing she had gained their cooperation before Melvin had been such a hero.

When she got back to town, she stopped at the locksmith's small building and went inside. The young man behind the counter smiled politely as she told him about her purse being stolen, and her keys had been inside. His uncle owned the place and came from a back room while she was listing the locks that needed rekeying immediately. "My business, my apartment, and my car all need to be secured." By the time they were through for the day, everything was rekeyed, and she felt much better. The cost was excessive, but she hoped her renter's insurance would cover at least part of it. While the men worked on the locks of her building, she went upstairs to the old apartment that had been vacant for years. When she'd bought the small building two years ago, she had plans to fix the place up to make it livable for herself to live in, but hadn't started doing anything more than painting the small place. She'd chosen a soothing blue for the living area, and a bright yellow for the kitchen. The bathroom was white. The bedroom was a complete change of decoration from the rest of the rooms. One wall was painted a turbulent dark bluish green, and the other three walls were murals with trees and bushes that she'd drawn and painted herself. The floor was a walnut stained hardwood, with brown and green rugs scattered around where she had left them. There was a dormer window that she'd installed louvered storm shutters on the inside for privacy too. The room appeared to be a place in a forest to her eyes, and she loved it.

There was a small balcony off the living room area that she planned to enclose with screening, for sitting outside on a warm summer day and relaxing, but hadn't gotten that far yet. Once David had moved in with her, this place had been forgotten while she'd struggled with the cost of keeping two of them in groceries and day-to-day living. Her business was thriving, since she was the only groomer in three counties. The two counties that surrounded this one were sparsely populated, and there wasn't enough work for most groomers to set up shop. So far she was kept busy. She could have hired someone to help her part-time, but until she was booked every day, all day, she was going to continue to be a one-woman show. She worked Monday thru Saturday and closed at noon on Saturday. When David came to live with her, he only showed up a few times to give baths while she trimmed hair and nails. He hated the little dogs and ferrets. When a twenty-two pound cat named Elmer came in, he laughed at him, and the cat knew it. He bit him, and David tried to hit the cat with a leash while it hid under the table where he had been thrown, and she'd had to intervene. That was the end of having a helper. The cat cried pitifully when she picked him up and checked to make certain he had no broken bones.

She was the product of a broken marriage, her father had no idea how to raise a baby girl, and her mother was so caught up in finding the new love of her life, she had no time for a whining child. She was foisted on her paternal grandparents for them to raise. Without the love and nurturing they had given her, she would probably be like David, hopefully she would be smarter, but she knew she would never have gone to college, or operate a business like she did. Her grandparents had never had a great deal of money, they lived paycheck to paycheck like most of the working class nowadays. Her beloved Grandma Geraldine, was diagnosed with lymphoma, cancer in the lymph nodes, and died within a few short months. Grandpa Rob died of a heart attack six months later. She always thought it was because he couldn't live without his spouse of fifty-six years, and died of a heart so broken, it couldn't be mended.

They'd left her the old Dodge, and their personal possessions, most of which were donated to the local homeless population, with the exception of a few items of jewelry that she kept locked up in a bank vault. After the run-in with David and his friends, she was happy she'd put the small gold earrings and necklace set, and her grandfather's heirloom gold pocket watch in the deposit box. She took the few thousand that was left after the funerals, and bought this place. A move she needed to make.

Her grandparents were gone, her life with Arlan had gone from tense to cheating, and his dominant side had grown into an abusive situation that she was ready to leave. A month after the funeral for her grandfather, she packed her belongings and left Arlan for good.

Now she was planning another move, and it felt right. She would save on gas money, and time too. Not to mention the rent and electric at the apartment. With the new keys, and the lack of access for someone to break into her apartment here, she would be as safe as possible. She could finally get a dog of her own. Melvin's intervention today reminded her that dogs were indeed protective to those they liked.

The apartment sliding door was repaired, and the new keys were in her hand, but for the first time in her life, she was afraid to enter her own home. No matter how she looked at it, someone could be waiting for her inside, she turned back to the parking lot and locked herself inside of her car. Now what was she going to do? She needed to sleep, and she needed a bath and food. Her protesting bladder was the deciding factor. She started the car and headed back downtown. There was an old couch and a bathroom in the apartment above her shop. She would face her fears in the light of day. Tonight she was opting for safety. As far as she knew, David didn't know about the quarters above the shop, and she should be able to park her car behind the building. Her plan was in place, so she drove to the nearest sandwich shop to use their bathroom and grab a sandwich.

As she entered the building, two loud motorcycles roared into the parking lot, and she bit her own hand to keep from screaming when one of the riders got off his bike and started to smash the windows of her car with a long pipe. He got to her headlights and she stopped biting her hand long enough to yell at him to stop. Her cell phone was in her hand before she knew she'd grabbed it from the side of her hip and she dialed 911. The laughter that echoed in the almost deserted lot was David's. The man with him was doing something behind the car that she couldn't see. The dispatch woman told her to stay in the building and away from the door.

She heard the sirens just minutes after the bikes left the parking lot. She was in the bathroom when the officer knocked on the door and asked if she was all right. She was embarrassed, but once the immediate threat had left, her bladder decided that it had waited long enough and she'd run into the tiled room and sat down just in time.

She came out of the room to see the cop chatting with the owner of the shop. When he saw her standing there, he walked her to her car, and shined his flashlight on it. The car that her grandfather had left to her, was beaten on the fenders until there were rippled lines where the top met the hood. There was no glass in the windows, or lights left intact. On the trunk the words "Yur Next Bitch" were spray painted in red.

"Where would you like to call to have the car towed to? We don't have an impound lot, so we usually call Gunner's Garage to take care of derelict vehicles, or vehicles that have been in an accident. They have a fenced in yard, and no one in their right mind would break into that place."

She nodded her head and he made the call. He offered to take her home, and she was thankful about that. He was a cop, he carried a gun. She would ask him to check out her apartment before she entered it, and if he gave her the all clear, she would lock herself inside and not come out until Monday.

The flatbed tow truck showed up, and a tall man with a red bandana over his head and a t-shirt advertising Gunner's Garage began to hook up the car. She had spoken with him before, he was the man who fixed the water pump a few months back. His name was, her memory drew a blank for a moment, John, yeah that was it. She should excuse her memory lapse due to the fact he was some pretty damn beautiful scenery to look at. His smile was just a little crooked, and his arms were nice and thick, and his hands, his hands were enough to fascinate her too. He was another wet panty inspiration. He was actually the first bald headed man that she'd ever fantasized about.

When the car was secured to the flatbed, the driver came over to her with a paper on a clipboard for her to sign, giving him permission to remove the vehicle and take it to the garage. He was grim faced and the first thing he said was, "What in the hell did you do to piss off the guy that did this? I keep this baby in shape for you to drive, and look at what happens. They don't fuckin' grow on trees you know, I told you it was a classic, and to be careful, remember?"

She grabbed the clipboard and scrawled her name on the bottom, shoved it back into his chest, and turned away, muttering to the cop, "You tell him." She stomped over to the cruiser and stood by the passenger door, waiting for Mr. Personality and the officer to finish talking. Why were all of the good looking men that had ties to Lucifer's Breed such assholes. It wasn't like she put up a damn sign saying "destroy me" next to the Swinger. The sound of a fire engine didn't register. This year had been dry, and they were all praying for rain to rescue the crops in the area. People didn't care when they tossed cigarette butts from their car windows. They were long gone before the hot ends of the cigarettes caught the dry grasses on fire.

She heard the police radio crackle and what sounded like code words to her, and looked up as the officer came running for the car. He unlocked the door and yelled, "Get in." She was happy to comply. It would be great to finally get to her apartment and… Her dream of a glass of wine and a hot bath was cut short by the officer driving fast through the streets of town.

"You own the pet grooming place on East Street?" A shiver of dread skimmed over her body.

They parked two blocks away from the fire. The tow truck parked behind them, and the driver got out and came to where they sat. She had already been pulled back when she tried to get out of the cruiser by the cop. So she stared at the ruins of her life, while they discussed the cause of the fire. "Molotov Cocktail" was the suspicion. And since she'd just reported her brother as one of the perps involved with her car being vandalized, and the fact he and his associates had roughed her feathers last night, David was their first suspect.

There was shouting and the sound of the roof collapsing inward, while people scrambled back from the top blocks falling onto the sidewalk. The gas company was digging furiously, trying to get to the shut-off under the sidewalk at the road. They would normally shut the gas off at a main valve, but her place was at the only break in the block, and the real threat was a natural gas explosion. They didn't have time to guess which end of the block the ancient lines connected. They heard shouts again, and a victory whoop, when the gas line was finally located, and disconnected.

She wanted to cry, no, she wanted David's neck between her fingers and thumbs. She wanted this to be a bad dream but, reality was staring at her, and she had no idea what to do about it.

# CHAPTER FOUR

Gunner wanted to nurse his arm where that damn dog bit him, but the vet said it would just be sore for a few days, and that he was lucky Melvin was only trying to scare him. "Sometimes the little dogs bite and let go, other times they keep it up when they are threatened or you piss them off. You caused the tearing when you jerked him up and he latched on hard to keep from falling."

When Baron and the rest of the guys finished laughing, they'd helped him clean up and called the vet, otherwise known as Doc, to the club. Baron asked the man to look at Melvin, "Just to make sure his teeth hadn't been pulled loose." He gave the little bastard a mint to "get the nasty taste of Gunner" from his mouth too.

Now that he was lying in his bed, thinking about Amelia, Gunner wanted to bust her ass, if for no other reason than being stupid. She couldn't really believe they would police their Prospects to the point of grounding them when they were naughty, could she? She was going to get a visit from him in a few days and he would try to explain that her brother had defected with his idol, Reeker. He wasn't the only Prospect that had illusions that weren't materializing. So far, the members had left the wannabes alone. Some of the members felt bad for Reeker. After all, he was just doing what he'd always done. His lying and the sneaky shit he was doing had gotten him shunned. He was excommunicated from the Breed. Any brother seen talking to him was in serious trouble, and nobody wanted that kind of trouble. Especially when it was the MC's top dog national president, Wolfman, who had issued the edict.

This time he'd been caught in the act by a living witness, a very believable witness. Since it was now confirmed that Reeker and his group were drugged and fried with it, the worse it looked on biker's period. The Breed might need to eliminate the problem altogether. Wolfman had insinuated their district had gone soft, but he couldn't see everything that they did either, and they liked it that way.

It was a daily struggle to follow the policies of Wolfman, and balance them with the club's original charter. The man didn't mind pissing in someone else's yard, neighbor or not. In his position, the yards and neighbors were always changing, so he didn't have to live in the same community year after year. Raising hell and establishing yourselves as kings of your territory was one thing, destroying the community your kids went to school was entirely different.

The past month had been a bitch for the home base here. Wolfman was running the circuit because there had been talk of replacing him. He figured he was going to make an example out of the defectors. Wolfy should have checked his back pockets before pulling the President of their club into his entourage. War aka Ward Hines, was not the run of the mill psychopath that Wolfman surrounded himself with. Until the night of the meeting with the Bastards MC, he had been the local Prez. Now

Baron was. Whoever had put his name up on the radar as a bodyguard for Wolfman, had to have known that War would not take the shit that Wolfman was famous for spreading around. They were all waiting to hear what the outcome would be.

Leaving Reeker alive had been a mistake. The kind of mistakes Wolfman had been doing a lot of lately. Jarl and his buddy, Mule, had been Nomads under Wolfman's direction. They had done some stupid shit, and got caught. And, like most rabid dogs, their owner had to put them down. How they got to Reeker and five other club members had never been established, but War was ready to take care of them himself when Wolfman showed up. Three years, it had taken three years to get enough information for a sanctioned action, and suddenly the old boy shows up on their doorstep. Something wasn't right, hopefully War would get to the bottom of it.

He fell asleep thinking about a pretty blonde with a prissy demeanor and a warm mouth.

*****

Waking up was a process for him. He had to get the morning business taken care of and as he was towel drying his hair, there was a knock on his door. He ignored the knock as he poured a cup of coffee into his favorite mug. When the person didn't go away, he jerked the door open.

John Handy was on the other side of the door and his heavy fist was raised to hit the door again. He lowered his arm and stepped inside. Gunner shrugged his shoulders, and shut the door behind his morning guest. "What's up?"

"I'm taking a leave to go hunting. I just wanted you to know that you need to find someone to cover my time for a while." He went into the kitchen area of the studio apartment and poured himself a cup of the mud Gunner called coffee.

"I got a call from Jimmy Wilson last night to pick up a vandalized car downtown. When I got there and saw the car," John shook his head and rubbed his face with both hands. "You know that old '71 Dodge with the 340 Auto that comes in for routine oil changes and stuff?"

Gunner thought for a minute, and nodded his head. That car was a particular favorite of John's, he had one back in the day, and he had good memories of the times. John took care of most of the older classic style cars that came in.

"Someone vandalized the survivor?" That was sacrilege.

John nodded and explained the extent of the damages. "If we can find the parts it will be a miracle. Anyway, I got her on the rollback, and while I was talking with Jimmy, he got a call about a fire and ran like hell for his car. The owner of the car was with him, and I thought it was kind of strange that he'd take someone on an emergency call like that, so I followed him." He took a large swallow of coffee and continued his tale. "The fire was downtown, and I pulled in behind the cruiser. The woman wanted to get out and Jimmy made her stay put, even threatened to put her in the cage if she didn't stay in the car. It turns out that her brother is the one who beat the shit out of the car, and Jimmy is pretty certain he's the one who firebombed the building too. The fucker already gave the woman shit the night before, and whatever she did to set him off, he has a hard-on to hurt her where it counts.

"When Jimmy mentioned they had been busy every night for the last week or so from violent shit happening, he let it slip that some punks were trying to start a new generation of biker thugs in the area. I know he was feeding me information, but we have been good for this town, so he figures we can help with the problem."

He finished his coffee and stood.

"I can see being pissed at your sister, I have one of them, and she is a nagging bitch at times, but no matter how pissed she makes me, I wouldn't vandalize her property like this little bastard has done. She couldn't even go home to her apartment. They know where she lives and spray painted threats on the car and her apartment door. Jimmy wouldn't let her get out of the car at the complex. He figured they might be watching, and try to reach out and touch her with firepower of a different kind this time. As far as I know, she slept at the station. I told Jimmy that I would see what I can find out about them.

"I wanted to let you know what I'll be doing so you can get one of the others to cover my shifts." He nodded his head again and headed for the door.

"Hang on a minute, John. You are not gonna believe this, but she showed up at the club yesterday bitching at Baron and me about her brother. She blames the Breed for allowing him to fall in with Reeker, and the drugs the kid is taking are our fault too. She is a snotty little twitch, but I agree, no one deserves to be shit on by her own brother like that. Grab another cup while I get dressed, and we'll roust Baron and a few of the others. This has gone way past a druggie looking for a handout from his sister."

* * * * *

Baron wasn't happy about walking into the police station. He'd tried to talk someone else into going, but no one volunteered. Knowing Oscar and Jimmy, she wouldn't be allowed to leave with another woman, so Myrtle was out too. Leech, Irish, and Chaucer waited with the bikes in the parking lot.

He'd been sleeping this morning when the bikes roared into his peaceful slumbers, and Melvin had begun to jump on him to get him out of bed. He'd no more than thrown on his jeans when the pounding on his door started and voices could be heard through the open window of his bedroom.

Gunner and Chaucer stood back and let the newest member of the group beat on Baron's door, they knew what would happen as soon as he stepped a foot over the threshold. Sure enough, the smiling man of seconds ago went sailing backwards out of the door he'd walked through. Gator landed on the dirt packed path, and he sat up holding his jaw, with a bewildered look on his face.

Chaucer leaned down and gave him a hand up. "Rule number one, don't beat on Baron's door more than twice, it makes him cranky if he has to hurry to make you stop. That love tap was to make sure you don't forget next time."

Gator was the last man to enter the house. Gunner grinned at him and shook his head. "Dumbass, next time wait a few before beating on a door. You were lucky it was Baron, Dino and Vern answer the door with a sawed off. Rebel and several others have pit bulls and shepherds. Even Myrtle has a damn Siamese cat that will slit your carotid artery if he gets to your neck."

John explained the evening's happenings, and someone handed Baron a mug of coffee. He looked up and saw his benefactor was Preacher, and he thanked him.

"So, let me get this straight. John wants to hunt down this kid because he vandalized a classic car, and as a side note, to add sweetness to the hunt, for the good of the community. Gunner thinks we should shelter the sister, the sister I might add, that blames us for her brother's drug use, and expects us to ground his ass and send him into rehab."

All ten heads nodded. "Okay, we go hunting."

Gator cleared his throat and asked for permission to speak. Most of the new Brothers who were still on a probationary status like he was, were too timid to speak up in a crowded room. He was more nervous not to. "I got this vibe two days ago from Lloyd. He was asking questions that I couldn't answer, mainly because I really don't know anything about a bag of yellow bling. That's what he called it. He said someone had the bag, and if I was to see it, he would split it with me. Then he started asking who to see about scoring some meth." He cleared his throat again, "I uh, I told him that the only guy I knew that was into shit like that was named Reeker, but he wasn't in the club anymore. We were having a few beers, and he kept asking questions, you know?"

Preacher smacked the younger man on the shoulder. "Boy, you did good. I might have to put you up for a vote sooner than we thought." He looked at Baron and got the nod. "You just keep being dumb. We're all a bunch of innocent sons-a-bitches, and don't you forget it..."

Melvin came through the room with something in his jaws. His short legs were eating up the run-through into the kitchen, and he came back through the room still running his little legs off. While the men talked strategy to capture the wannabes, he made his circuit three more times. It wasn't until Leech went to refill his coffee mug that anyone actually paid attention to Melvin's odd behavior. All they could hear was the man's laughter. Everyone trouped into the kitchen and had to stifle their own amusement while Baron began to curse.

Melvin was standing guard over four kittens at his food dish. He had one side of his teeth bared toward Leech. The kittens didn't know what to do with the medium sized chunks of dog chow, and were mewling pitifully in hunger. It was obvious the kittens hadn't been fed in a while. One was actually swaying where it stood.

Melvin would only let Baron and Burger near the kittens while Fester and Jake raided the fridge for milk and an egg to stir together and warm for a few seconds in the microwave. Gunner called Doc.

Burger kept dipping his finger in the egg and milk mixture and tapping the tip of his finger to the tip of each kitten's nose. They licked the wetness off, and once they learned the offending stuff tasted like food they opened their little mouths, looking for more. Baron handed kittens to Fester and Jake to help feed the little creatures, while he went to finish dressing for the day. Melvin sat on the bed watching him.

"You are ruining your rep, Mel, what kind of a badass fucker takes in half dead strays like that. All I can say is don't make a habit of it. One day you're tearing up Gunner's arm and the next you rescue a litter of kittens, I'm beginning to think you're bipolar or something." He sighed and put the little guy's cut on him. "We're not keeping them here, man, I have enough to do to keep you and me taken care of. I don't have time to mess with those fur balls. Tell you what, we'll take them to the club and Myrtle can take care of them, that sound okay to you?"

Melvin didn't have much to say but he trotted out of the room, and stayed by his side until they mounted up for the ride to the club. He watched each kitten being stuffed into the shirts of four men and seemed satisfied they were being treated well.

The club's bitches made a big fuss over the multi-colored kittens while Doc checked them out. They were given antibiotics and one of the women took off for the store to buy litter and supplies.

Baron asked for volunteers to go fetch Amy, and the men scattered like roaches when the lights flipped on. He was lucky to snag the three that he did. "Bunch of chicken shit fuckers, I see how you are."

47

*****

Oscar Lime was sitting at the front desk in the small office, and Amy was leafing through an old magazine. The poor old man was tickled to see someone walk through the door. Baron sat in the visitor's chair, slumping and chatting with the chief for a few minutes before getting to the point of his visit.

"I know some of what's been happening around here, I'm here to tell you that me and the club will be happy to help in any way we can to turn those troublemakers over to you. We have feelers out, and we will keep you in the loop if we get any good information. We can't have shit like they're doing, going around in our town."

Amy listened to the conversation. The big man sure had the police chief wrapped up. He seemed to be agreeing to anything the biker said. She stopped wondering what he would look like without clothes when she heard her name mentioned.

"As soon as Gus gets back from taking statements about the robbery down by the highway, we plan to escort Miss Selters to her apartment so she can be comfortable while we look for her brother and his cohorts. I admit to being nervous leaving her there, but we don't have the budget for a safe house or an extra officer to stay with her, and she has been nagging the hell out of me to let her go home."

It irritated her, the way these men spoke about her circumstances. Her mother and the Judge were cruising in the Bahamas, or she could have called them to help her with the problems David was causing her.

Oscar leaned forward to whisper, "They left a dead cat on the stoop of her apartment and threatening words spray painted on the wall. She's meat if she goes back there."

Baron came over to her and told her to get her purse. "Why? The officers will take me home, you heard the chief, they will patrol often, and I will keep the doors locked." There, she told him, she stood up for herself. He needed to know she wasn't some shrinking violet. At five seven, and a hundred sixty pounds, she wasn't a small woman, but standing in front of him, made her feel almost tiny. He had to be a foot taller than she was, and his shoulders and arms were thickly muscled. If he was a skinny man, she wouldn't be so attracted, or so she told herself. Remembering the other men at the group's hangout caused her to lie to herself about that. Four of them could have made her sigh if it had been in different circumstances that they'd met. Baron or his friend, Gunner, would have been her first choices, if she'd had to choose.

# CHAPTER FIVE

"Look, lady, it's like this, you blame the Breed for your brother's actions, we blame Reeker. You are a target. We have voted, you are coming with me to the clubhouse. You'll be safe there, and it will give us a chance to find the little bastard and his mentor. Once the cops have him, we are done, so don't expect anything more than that from us. Get your shit and let's go. I have things to do."

Her "shit" consisted of her purse. She didn't even have a change of underwear, and she wasn't going anywhere with him voluntarily. She shook her head no, but that had no effect on him other than to give her a narrowed eyed look and she couldn't believe it when he jerked his head at the chief and the man got up and left the room. Baron grabbed her arm, pulling her to her feet, and she found herself over his shoulder heading toward the door. She kicked her feet and pushed herself up on the wide perch, but got a hard smack on her thigh for her trouble. She tried again, and got a harder smack on her ass. She grabbed a hunk of his thick hair and gave it a hard yank. "Let me go you overgrown Yeti, I don't need you to take me anywhere."

Baron figured he'd been nice long enough, she got a free pass yesterday, mainly because he had been laughing at Gunner too hard to catch her before she'd left. He walked over to an empty desk, and sat on it. He pulled her down from his shoulder and she let go of his hair, probably thinking he was going to let her go. He held onto her and as soon as she was in the right position, he pushed her down over his lap, grabbed a fistful of her hair, and laid his big hand on her ass in a meaningful way—hard. He began smacking her jean clad ass, and telling her to behave in a stern voice.

"Get over yourself, little girl, I'm not some pussy boy that gives a damn about your sensitive feelings, and if you don't stop that goddamn screeching, I'll gag you." That shut her up, at least for a minute. "You are going to get your happy ass on my bike, and you're going to stop bitching long enough to see that this is the best plan to keep you safe, and your brother caught. You came to us, remember?" He gave her three more hard smacks for good measure. He had to tell his prick to knock it off, the fucker was waking up in a big way, and he didn't particularly want to be riding with a hard-on. He let her stand up and headed for the door.

She rubbed her tender butt cheeks, and slowly walked out of the building. Her mind was shifting through her emotions and she was afraid her common sense was going to win this round. She truly had nowhere to go that was safe from David, and if this offer of shelter hadn't come, she would be a sitting duck at her apartment. There was the incentive of being around so many sexy men, so at least she would have something to keep her busy while she was with them. It could be worse, instead of watching muscular jean clad asses walk by, she could be stuck here, watching the chief's beer belly expand.

He kicked the motor starter thing, and gave her that narrow eyed look again, so she hiked her leg over the bike and sat behind him. There was nothing to hang on to, and she had no idea where to put her feet either. His arm reached back, grabbed her leg, and guided it to a peg on the side, just above the long shiny exhaust pipes, so she looked down on the other side and set her other foot on that one too. He yelled, "Hang on," and she had to grab at his waist to keep from falling off the big machine. She gave Chaucer a little hand wave as they passed him sitting on his bike, waiting for them to pass. He might have smiled, but she had to grab on to her anchor so fast she hadn't had a chance to notice.

Twenty minutes later they turned into the driveway of the club. She was so excited that she almost fell on her ass after she pulled her leg over the small patch of leather she'd been sitting on and balanced on her toes. She kept her hand on Baron's shoulder until she got her bearings and could stand with confidence. "I want one of these, I want to learn how to drive one. What kind of bike should I look for, being a beginner, I know I should start out with a smallish one, but I loved that ride."

She was grinning at him and he had to smile at her enthusiasm. A few of the old ladies had their own scooters and could give her tips on what the best ones to learn on might be. His first bike had been a 350 Rice grinder. At fourteen, he'd been over six feet tall, and the smaller bikes made him feel like a bear on a tricycle. At sixteen, he'd graduated to his first Triumph 750 Trident, and the wreckage of that one still sat in his pole barn.

"You can ask Vern's old lady, she rides. Come on, let's get you situated."

Melvin was excited to see Amy walk in the door. She was equally happy to see a friendly face, even if it was a furry one with dog breath. In the far corner of the room, a small gathering of women in various degrees of skimpy clothes were giggling and cooing to something small enough to be held in the palms of their hands. She walked closer and saw the tiny orange, black, and brown body of one of the kittens. It couldn't be very old, unless she was looking at the runt.

Myrtle came up behind her and introduced her to the Bitch Pack. "The one holding the kitten there is Charm, next to her is Hightits. Friendly is the one with the red hair, and the rest are Angel, Lovey, Freddie, and Ducky. Bernie and Henri are shopping right now. They will be back tonight, so you can meet them then. Ladies, this is Amy, she is a guest, not one of the Bitches or round heeled party sluts, so be friendly, she's not the competition."

Every one of the women smiled at her except the one Myrtle said was named Hightits. There must be a problem there, she didn't know what her problem was, and hoped she wouldn't be here long enough to find out. She'd seen that look before when she had walked in on Arlan and his fuck buddy screwing on her bed while she'd been at work all day. The woman hadn't lasted more than a few days as far as she knew, but this Hightits could certainly match the other one in dirty looks. The only way to deal with women like them was to ignore them, or beat their asses. Unfortunately, Amy wasn't confident enough to beat the woman physically, so she chose to ignore her.

Myrtle gave her the nickel tour of the place. "Bathrooms are scattered around, and if you don't want someone walking in on you, make sure you use the lock on the door. This is the bar where everybody congregates." They walked through the bar and into another room with tables and chairs. "This is the room where we set up a buffet on the weekends and it's pretty much grab and go. We don't do fancy, but the kitchen is through there and it has everything you might need to fix some simple meals if you're any kind of cook. In the back there are a few rooms for privacy if anyone is feeling the need. The Office is back there, but if you plan to check the single rooms out, don't make the mistake of coming back here with any of the men. You've been warned. You cross the line of this room and the hallway with anyone, don't come screaming rape later."

She was left to her own devices when Myrtle got a call on her cell.

Charm and Ducky came racing through the door and Ducky peeked around the doorjamb to make sure they'd escaped whoever was following them. Charm grabbed Amy by the arm and pulled her into the kitchen with Ducky following close behind. They continued out of the building through the backdoor, onto a covered eating area. She hesitated to call it a patio, picnic tables and a huge fuel oil tank that had been cut in half, and had blackened sides, didn't look like her idea of something as fancy as a patio. An old fridge sat next to the building that Ducky got three beers from, then she brought them, and a bowl of boiled eggs still in the shell to the table Charm had selected for them.

Charm was a busty brunette with huge brown eyes, and an infectious smile. Ducky was a tiny redhead with light golden skin and cinnamon speckles over every inch of her bared skin. They both appeared to be in their mid-twenties, and invited her to conspire with them against Gunner.

As Charm said, "He is such a bastard, did you hear that him and Leech have been warning some of the guys that us bitches are trying to trap them into locking down for the next eighteen years. He didn't bother to tell them that not all of us feel we need to snag one of them anytime soon. I ain't settling down until one of these motherfuckers proves he's worth the sacrifice."

Amy was smiling with the girls, even she felt they'd been falsely accused, "So how am I supposed to help you? I barely know Gunner or Leech."

Ducky held up a finger for Amy to hold on a moment while she finished swallowing the egg in her mouth. She slugged half a beer down and smiled as she burped. "Oops, sorry for that. You, our new acquaintance, and most bosom of friends, get to interview our prospective old men. We will use you to ask questions while we are entertaining the guys tonight. Things like income, do they have homes, do they like kids. You know, shit like that."

Charm was sharing her grin with the girls, "You can't act all prissy either, you gotta be aggressive, 'cause I can be pretty distracting when I'm giving a guy head. The men figure they're going to get all the goodies without having to share the wealth for a few weeks. I don't plan on going without tonight, so you have to ask why they are such selfish lovers, shit like 'hey, I thought bikers were 'spossed to be such badass lovers. Not a bunch of selfish pricks.'" She must have seen the look of disbelief on Amy's face.

"Now you don't have to stand over us and score our techniques, just sit around the room in different spots, asking questions or making comments. You want to help us right? Even Hightits would be grateful if you agree and we wanted her to know. She has her sights on being an old lady, she wants Gunner and Baron."

Amy felt a disturbance in her chest. "If she wants them to fight over her, I won't lift a lip to ask anything on her behalf. I hate it when women try to pit men against each other." Her companions laughed at her declaration.

"You are gonna be a fun one to have around here. Gunner and Baron like to share, they wouldn't fight over a woman, they're pretty famous for wearing a bitch out. We haven't been the meat in their particular sandwich, or some of the other shit they are known for, kinky shit. Give me a straight up fuck, I can even enjoy taking it in the ass once in a while." Charm grinned, "I wouldn't object to peeking in on them while they are doing the kinky shit though."

"Yeah, from what Caroline used to say about them," she fanned herself, "they used to do all kinds of shit to her and she loved it. After about a year or so, she kept bitching they weren't enough, she

56

wanted something more. Can you imagine? I still look at Baron and imagine him fucking her in the cunt and Gunner's fat prick fucking her ass at the same time. She loved it, she told me that it was something every woman should experience at least once."

Ducky finished her second egg, and what was left in her bottle of beer, and laughed. "Fuck yeah, I might try it just to say I did. I saw her blowing them off one night and I might be brave enough to try taking one of them, and say, maybe Skids. I'd be worried they would split me open like a peach."

Amy wondered if she was being hazed, like college or something. They led her into a doublewide trailer about a hundred feet from the backdoor. She fell asleep on the sofa while the ladies got ready for the evening. She never heard Angel and Freddie walk in the door.

An argument over someone's red heels woke her from a deep sleep. She sat up and ran her hands through her curly hair. "I'm sorry, I must have passed out, sleeping at the police station was not the easiest thing in the world to do. The officer offered to let me sleep in a cell, but for some reason that seemed as if I was the bad guy, and I was the one in the right."

Angel sat in the chair opposite where she was sitting and questions started coming her way. "What's your story anyway? We don't get visitors like you here you know. Did you have to do the splits when you rode with Baron on his hog? Caroline always said she had to practically do them just to get her legs on the pegs. Are you replacing

Caroline? I gotta tell you, Hightits ain't gonna like that at all. Can you cook? It would be great if we had another bitch that could cook here. Bernie does most of the cooking, but goulash is getting old after two years."

Amy blinked at her. Was she high? How could anyone talk that fast and be understood. Geez, she tried to answer the questions in order, but couldn't remember them all.

"Hi, um, my brother was one of the Prospects for the club here. He hooked up with a guy that was so bad even your club tossed him out on his ass. I refused to give him money, his buddy wanted to have sex with me and their other nasty little friend, they vandalized my car, burned down my business, and have threatened my life.

"As for the other stuff, no I didn't have to do the splits, I was a gymnast in school, I would know if I had to do those. Ah, uh, no I am not a replacement, or substitute for anyone. Yes, I can cook, not fancy stuff, I can make other things than goulash, but I like goulash, and since I haven't eaten since sometime last night, I could eat a damned cow right now. I haven't had a shower since, hmm, maybe night before last? I didn't get a chance to even grab a change of clothes." She yawned again and saw that she had all four women starring at her. "What?"

Forty-five minutes later she stood in front of the full length mirror on the back of the bathroom door and was surprised the woman staring back at her looked young, carefree and dare she say—sexy? She wore a belly baring half t-shirt with the hemline tucked under the shelf bra's band. The neckline of the shirt was gone and split in a deep v down her chest. She wasn't exactly flat chested to begin with, and the bra and shirt made her breasts look much larger. The excuse for shorts let the bottom cheeks of her ass flash as she flexed her legs, and rode so low on her hipbones that she was afraid they would fall off her ass if she moved too much.

*This is one time you can be thankful for your wide ass, thank you, Grandma Selters.* Her feet were covered in leather half boots that made the outfit complete. Freddie did her make-up and gave her smoky smudged eyes. Her lips had a natural pout to begin with, now that they were outlined in a dark cherry lip stain, she wanted to blow everyone in the place a kiss. Ducky tried to tame her mop of curls, but the spirals resisted her efforts, and they gave up on the idea.

Charm grinned when she saw her. "Oh boy, Ol' Hightits is gonna be pissy tonight. You clean up good, Amy."

# CHAPTER SIX

She thanked them all and did a clumsy curtsey, "Thank you, Fairy Godmothers." The women made their way back to the club. The kitchen was a disaster. Someone had dumped bags of chips and other junk food. There were three empty pizza boxes, two large take out buckets with nothing but bones and grease left inside.

Amy could have cried. She was so hungry she was ready to snatch one of the potato chip bags and run to a corner.

The door opened before they got to it, to walk out of the room, and two Prospects and Baron walked in carrying more pizza and another bucket of chicken. Preacher came in behind him with a large cardboard box filled with lettuce leaves and cherry tomatoes. Other men and women brought bowls and bags with some form of edibles. Chaucer and Jake brought in beat up tin foil pans filled with grilled corn and unidentifiable chunks of meat that he had roasted over coals. Whatever it was, it smelled delicious.

She stood back, not knowing the pecking order when it came to who ate when around here. She knew she must be drooling but when the horde of hungry club members left the room with paper plates filled with food, she stepped up to get a plate for herself. It appeared that Baron had forgotten his guest as soon as he'd dropped her with Myrtle today. She got the plate, but couldn't find a single utensil, walked along the table and was shocked to see that all remaining food needed a spoon or fork to eat it with. She hated coleslaw, and there was a half of a bowl sitting there. The two cherry tomatoes that were left didn't begin to fill the ache in her stomach. Even the pizza had been snatched down to a couple of stray pepperonis.

She walked into the meeting/dining room and didn't see Baron, so she went into the lounge. He was sitting with a plate heaped with food on the table in front of him, and talking to Gunner and a young couple. The woman was obviously pregnant, and her old man sat close beside her.

She wove her way to the plate of food she'd zeroed in on, and when she was within reach, snagged a chicken leg from Baron's stash. He turned his head and frowned at her, but she gave him the same look he'd given her earlier, before she sank her teeth into the tender meat. She watched him watching her devour the small piece of meat, she tossed the bone next to his plate and swiped a slice of pizza next. When she straightened up and looked at him, she nodded her thanks and bit into the gooey cheesy treat. She turned away to go to the bar and ask for a cola to wash her stolen dinner down. Someone laughed behind her, but let them, she'd finally gotten something to soothe her stomach's demands.

Freddie was standing at the bar watching her approach and grinned. "I thought you were puttin' us on when you said you were a gymnast, but the way you move proves that you can balance really good in those fuck-me heels. Can you work a pole?"

Amy asked for a beer instead of a cola, she didn't want to act differently than the rest of the women in the room, and from what she could see, most of them were drinking beer or wine coolers. Only a few were drinking sodas. She took a couple of long pulls on the bottle and handed it to Freddie, "Let's see if I remember how it's done." Angel was working on the pole on the left, and the music had just gone from a banging discordant sound, to something that made a woman's inner slut want to move her hips to the beat. She wasn't sure if it was the outfit, the music, or the challenge that made her grab the shining chrome steel pole and swing around it. She grinned at Angel and they synced the movements of their hips for a few beats, then she began playing with the pole. She held onto the pole, moving to the beat of the music for the duration of the song without her heels touching the floor, until the last note. Her right leg was up along the pole, and her left leg was supporting her weight, in a standing split. She and Angel grinned as they finished their workout and Freddie laughed with them as they hopped off the miniscule platforms. She was clapping and fanning herself with her hand, telling them how hot that had been to watch.

"I fuckin' swear to Yani, that was so damned hot I wanted to join you girls, and I don't mean dancing on those metal poles. I know Angel works out with one for exercise, but that wasn't what you were doing on that thing."

Amy was feeling the adrenalin still coursing through her veins from her working the pole, it had been years since she touched one. She laughed.

"You know how you girls were making fun of the way I talk? I was raised by very proper southern grandparents. I also went to college, and they didn't have the money to send me there. I told them I got grants and scholarships to pay the tuition, but the truth was, I worked a pole in a strip club downtown for four years. I got my degree, and quit dancing, but at least I didn't have any big loans to pay for when I graduated."

John Handy pulled Angel off her feet, and carried her over his shoulder toward the back. Freddie waved at the grinning Angel as she bounced on his shoulder, and waved back. She patted his ass and they saw his hand land on hers in return.

Freddie asked for tips on how to get her legs to stretch like Amy's did, so she pulled a chair from a nearby table where two greybeards were sitting and found a small space to show her how to keep one foot flat on the chair and stretch the other leg out to make the muscles more elastic. She spied Gunner watching them and waved him over to where they were.

"I hope you won't mind helping me show Freddie here how to stretch her thigh muscles and tendons. I can probably ask one of the Prospects if you don't want to help." He gave her a growl and sat.

"Go ahead, do your worst, just make sure I don't get one of those heels in the head. And you are gonna owe me, so don't bitch when I decide to collect."

Amy smiled at him, "I'm rewarding you enough with this dance, men used to pay the management two bills to get this, and I always got good tips." She heard the Kid Rock song come on and grinned. "You just sit back and try not to fall asleep now."

Her hips started pumping and her arms circled his neck. He felt her breathe on his neck below his ear and felt the hairs on the back of his neck begin to stand. By the time her long leg raised up and hooked his neck, pulling his head down with his face almost touching her denim clad pussy, he could feel the pre-cum leaking onto the tip of his cock. With the last thirty seconds of the song, her leg came up from behind him and hooked his neck in the bend of her knee. His head was bent back and she lowered her face to his, giving him the impression that she was going to kiss him. She stopped a mere whisper away, made a kissing sound with her pursed lips, and let his head go back in a natural position. The music had stopped and she was heading for the bathroom before he knew she was no longer there.

Gunner took his time standing up and going back to the table where Baron was sitting. He was still hard as hell and he was vowing to himself that she was going to have his cock buried somewhere in her body tonight, the longer she made him wait, the harder he planned to fuck her. He looked at Baron and could tell the performance hadn't gone unnoticed by him either.

"If you don't plan to take her to the farm, tell me now, I'll fuck her here or wherever I can catch the little bitch. She did that on purpose and left me sitting with a damn hard-on and she is going to take care of it if I have anything to say about it. I'm just waiting for her to strut her ass out here again."

Baron watched the pole dancing and thought about her doing the splits like that on his pole. When she showed Freddie those stretches, he'd been ready to give her a ride. When she'd straddled Gunner without touching him, and wrapped that leg around his neck, he thought for sure Gunner was going to take a bite at that pussy, clothed or not. That last little thing she'd done with her leg around his neck, had him ready to take a bite. Her crotch was turned up and almost in his face, and he was in complete agreement with Gunner. The scared sister demanding they deal with her brother had been replaced by a dick teasing bitch, and she was slated to be the entertainment for the evening. They waited for her to come out of the bathroom.

*****

Amy grabbed a handful of paper towels and ran half of them under the faucet, before going into one of the stalls and hooking the door shut. She cleaned herself as well as she could, and used the dry towels to dab any remaining moisture. It wasn't the first time she'd gotten horny while dancing, the erotic dancing in itself was orgasm inducing, because you had to have sex on your mind to do a good job. Muscles stretched and flowed easier and more naturally when your intent was to arouse a partner, or more accurately a client who was forced to keep his hands to himself, while she did everything, moved in every way to entice a sexual feeling from him.

From the sight of the lump under his jeans, she could be proud of her dance being so successful. The last look in his eyes made her nervous. She'd seen men with flared nostrils and clenched jaws before, yet none that looked like Gunner, or that drew her like he did. She'd pulled her leg from his throat and looked up to see Baron's blue eyes staring at her with intent. She felt his eyes as she almost ran into the bathroom. Hopefully they would be engaged in sex with one of the other women when she composed herself, or she would be again tempted into teasing one or both of them. She was acting totally out of character in this place. Being with those girls and sharing make-up tips and just being one of a group of women had felt good. It made her want to continue to be one of them, so she pushed her reservations aside and let loose for the first time in years.

She exited the stall and was rearranging her breasts in the bra when the door opened and Hightits and Bernie walked in. "Hello, ladies," was met with a grim smile from Bernie. Hightits looked hostile, so she tried a different track. "I haven't exercised that much in years, my legs are going to hurt like hell tomorrow." All that speech got her was a pissed off blue eyed brunette advancing toward her with intent to do great bodily harm, if the rising hands and bent fingers were any indication of things to come. She held up a hand in front of her, and extended her own arm. "Personal space, lady, I don't know what your problem is, but you need to back the fuck off."

66

"Who the fuck do you think you are coming in here and acting like some kind of dance queen screwing with my man like that?" The slap to Amy's face as Hightits shoved past her extended arm stung.

She wanted to play it that way then? *Let's hope you remember how this is done.* She hadn't been in a fight since her pole dancing days and a married man's wife found him in the bar, watching her dance. This woman wasn't going to listen to reason. She was proved right when the names started flying and Hightits raised her hand to slap her again. "Oh no, you had one free pass, I'm not letting you use me to take your frustration out on. If you're pissed at your man, take this shit out on him, he never said a word about you when he sat his ass in that chair." She didn't bother with slapping and hair pulling like the other woman was doing, Amy belted her in the mouth with her fist. Bloody lips usually stopped a girl fight, but her opponent was too blinded by rage to worry about a few drops of blood, and kept yanking her hair.

Bernie stood by the door with her weight keeping it blocked against intruders. She didn't particularly care who won the fight, but she was trying to make sure that no one jumped in for either side. The blonde was giving Hightits a run for her money, and when her knee connected with the brunette's bottom jaw, it was lights out and a new Bitch Queen was born. Of course this woman wouldn't be hanging around for long, but for now, she won the fight.

Amy turned on the cold water and using both hands, rinsed the nasty scratch on her cheek. Her hair was beyond finger combing, and her knuckles on her right hand were bleeding from Hightits teeth connecting with them. She stood and looked down at the woman on the floor and had to stifle the urge to kick the ever living shit out of her as she lay there. If it wasn't for that small opening where she'd been able to raise her knee, it could have ended with her laid out instead of the other woman. She stared at Bernie, daring her to start some more shit, but the woman raised her hands in the air and stepped from the door.

"Not my fight."

She didn't bother to look to see who had been watching the bathroom door. Anyone in the room could have heard the screams and yelling coming out of the echoing space, even with the flimsy door shut. She stomped over to the bar and asked the strange little man for her purse that Myrtle had stashed under the bar for her when she'd first come in today. She asked the man to give her a phone book and when he plopped a ratty old directory in front of her, she thanked him, he ignored her and went about his business.

She found a cab company in the book and hoped that it was still open for business. Thankfully her phone was still charged up enough to make a call and she began to punch in the numbers to connect with her ticket out of this place, she was going back to her apartment tonight, tomorrow she would buy a gun for protection. The idea scared the hell out of her, but if that's what it took to be safe, she would do it.

She brought the phone up to her ear and her hand was taken from behind and raised up to Baron's ear. She stared at him wondering what his problem was until she saw the scowl on his face and he said, "Wrong number." Her phone was pried out of her hand and he grabbed her purse and tossed the phone inside. His hand went to her jaw and pulled her around to face him so he could get a good look at the long red scratch, and the darkening bruises on her cheek. Gunner stepped close to see the injury too.

"I've had enough protection from the members of Lucifer's Breed, I want to go home to my apartment. Since your woman has expressed her displeasure with my presence, I think it's best if I call a cab. I actually thought you men were at least faithful to your own, according to that woman, you and Gunner belong to her, and I am a fat assed cow that Gunner wanted to play with. Men that do that kind of thing make me sick, and from what I've heard from the Bitch Pack, you are all a bunch of selfish lovers who are only interested in getting your own pleasures. Why a woman would want to fight to keep a man like that escapes me, let alone two of you. If you get your rocks off having women fight over you, I'm not so sure if you are worth fighting over anyway." She realized that most of the people in the room could hear what she was saying due to her voice raising while she told the two big men what she thought of their actions. She tried to calm down a bit as she continued in a more normal tone.

"If the attack in the bathroom is any indication of things to come, I can sleep better knowing who wants to harm me at my place. At least he has a twisted reason for his hate. His is personal, and you can bet your overgrown asses that I am buying a gun tomorrow. I'm not hiding from anybody again, I'll protect myself, and you and your band of crazies can kiss my fat cow ass." She snatched her purse back from him and stomped to the front door. Gunner stepped in front of her and she lost her ladylike façade.

"Get out of my way, you lowlife. I left your woman on the bathroom floor with a sore jaw, she might have a hard time sucking your selfish pencil dick off for a few days, but she'll live. You can cheat on her with one of the other women. They can't very well tell you no, now can they?" She stepped around him and hit the door fast.

# CHAPTER SEVEN

Leech sat in his chair with Charm between his thighs, she was grinning, he would swear she was making giggle sounds instead of moaning in the pleasure he thought she should be feeling from sucking his cock. Amelia's words of disdain hit him. So the Bitch Pack felt the men were all a bunch of selfish lovers? He almost always thanked them for whatever kind of fucking they engaged with him, afterwards. Even for a simple blowjob. He did his duty most of the time and made sure the woman got her orgasm too. From the way Charm was acting you'd think she never got to enjoy his cock. He pulled her head off his near bursting prick and yanked her shorts off her, and fingered her for a minute to get her juices flowing to make his path easier for both of them. He pulled her down on his cock and kept his finger on her clit while she pumped her hips up and down over him. Her moans were real this time, and he enjoyed hearing them.

Hightits opened the bathroom door and stumbled out into the room with a bloody lips and a swelling jaw. No one was looking at her, it was as if she didn't exist. When she woke up to find herself alone on the concrete floor, she could smell where someone had puked on and never bleached the floor to disinfect it from probably last weekend. She'd gotten mad at the rest of the women for not backing her up. For the first time in a long time, she felt completely alone. No one came looking for her, Bernie had left the room, and was doing God knows what. No one cared about her. She could have been dead on the floor and no one would have even bothered to check her pulse. Her reflection in the mirror horrified her. No amount of cold water would make the swelling on her lip go down, and the swelling jaw was beginning to turn a dark purple. She stared at herself for several long minutes. She was thirty-two years old, and had nothing but a set of silicone breasts and a worn out soul to show for it. Maybe it was time for her to make a change. The few men she'd developed a fondness for didn't want her. They'd enjoyed her skills as a fuck buddy, but that was about it.

Her name was Sylvia Castor. It had been so long since someone had called her Sylvia that it was a surprise when someone actually spoke her name. "Your name is Sylvia Castor, you are thirty-two years old, and you just woke up on a concrete floor with bruises that you invited on yourself," she told her reflection. A new feeling of change was trying to shove itself to the surface. "Is this what you want to do for the rest of your life?" The answer to that question gave her the guts to walk out of the bathroom to face the ridicule and laughter. Let them laugh, it would be the last time she would set herself up to fail. She had plans to make, a life to find that didn't include her current situation, and she needed a hot shower to disinfect her hair and face from the nasty floor. When she saw no one worried about her enough to laugh or make comments, it just solidified her determination to change her life. She left through the backdoor and ignored the people at the picnic tables as she made her way home.

Amy was at the gate, and the rough looking men were giving her a hard time about leaving. "Look, lady, I just do my job. No one told me to let you leave yet, and until they do, you can stick around with me and Irish. We don't mind having a pretty woman hanging out with us, do we Irish?"

She was so frustrated and still pissed about the fight and her encounter with Gunner that she could hardly stand herself, let alone two more Neanderthals. The sounds of two powerful motors didn't distract her from stomping her foot in an effort to lose some of her anger. When Baron pulled his bike up next to her at the gate, he told her to get on, he would take her home. She stared at him a few seconds and nodded. She lifted her leg over the small space behind him and settled in for the ride home. Hopefully he would insist on searching her apartment before leaving her by herself.

The air was much colder than it had been in the daylight for the ride here. The skimpy outfit she was wearing was no protection for her bare skin. Her hands crept up under his leather jacket, and she snuggled closer to his back with her head tucked down behind his thick shoulder. He slowed the bike and made a turn, but she kept tucked down from the wind. When he stopped the bike, she finally looked up and wondered where they were. There was a beautiful log home from what she could see, and as the other bike that was following them pulled in next to them, she could see that Gunner was driving that one. So much for her lightened mood.

"You said you were taking me home, this isn't my apartment building, I've never been here before." He dismounted but she sat where she was. He couldn't seriously believe that she was going to continue to be fucked with like this. Her libido was working overtime still and the knowledge that Baron had brought her to this place didn't bode well for her peace of mind.

"You assumed I meant your home, this one is mine. Come on let's get inside, I can see you shivering from the cold."

She followed him to the door. All the way thinking about how stupid she'd been not paying attention to where they'd headed when they left the clubhouse. Gunner stomped in behind them. Melvin almost knocked her down from the fuck me heels she was wearing when he saw her. She couldn't help but give him a bit of loving, and praise for his beautiful little self. "There's my little man, you are looking so good, look at this little guy. Are you a good boy?"

Baron called him and made him go outside to take care of his business, then told her to follow Gunner. She didn't want to follow the silent man anywhere. Since she didn't want to anger either man further tonight, she followed down a short flight of steps and into a large room with what appeared to be workout equipment. That explained the thick muscles. Riding a motorcycle and swilling beer all of the time wasn't the kind of lifestyle that inspired muscles like Baron's, or even Gunner's.

Watching Gunner remove his jacket and t-shirt reminded her that she'd been feeling a lot friendlier to him two hours earlier than she did now. It had been too long since she'd been around a real man, is all that had been. Maybe she should seriously look around for a boyfriend or maybe even a fuck buddy until she found someone who could or would give her the kind of sex she needed. Arlan hadn't understood anything but abuse. Her needs were for a bit of pain with the pleasure. Most men had no idea how to give her what she needed. Asking for what she wanted was always misinterpreted, so she gave up on trying. Her e-reader was filled with books about her kink, but real life men didn't have a clue.

She wondered what Baron or Gunner would say if they saw her pierced nipples. They'd probably say something stupid and piss her off even more.

"Here's a bathroom, you can take a shower too. There's a robe behind the door if you don't want to use a towel when you're done. Baron will be down in a few minutes, so if anything else is needed he can get it for you."

She was happy that he was being at least polite. "Thank you, Gunner, I think I owe you an apology for at least part of what I said earlier. You don't make me sick, the circumstance did. If I'd known you belonged to that woman, I wouldn't have chosen you for that lap dance. I learned to dance while I was in college, it made paying the bills easier, and the lap dances were something that made a lot of money. They bought the books and paid the rent. Some days the tips I got from a dance meant whether I'd eat bologna or Ramon noodles for a week. Tonight I lost my head and cut loose a bit too much, and showed off some of my old skills. I apologize for causing you problems with your girlfriend."

His mouth was open, in surprise? She'd swear it had been emotion she saw, but it was probably weariness that gave her that impression. Maybe he wasn't used to women apologizing to him. Who knew what was in the head of a man, she was too weary to try to figure it out tonight. There was no lock on the bathroom door, but she wasn't worried about them disturbing her. They were probably working out and keeping those muscles she saw covering Gunner's chest in top condition. She would love to get a chance to look closer at the tattoos that decorated his torso. The problem with getting that close, her tongue might want to trace the lines and curves on each picture. She decided to go ahead and take a shower, the warmth of the house was welcome, but she would warm up faster in the shower than waiting for her body temp to rise without some help from hot water.

The hot water had done its job and made her feel warm and even woke her up a bit. She towel dried her hair and found the robe to cover her bare body. The robe hung down to her ankles and she was sure it had to belong to Baron to be this big on her. She opened the door expecting to see two sweaty guys working out for her eyes to feast on, and her inner slut to enjoy fantasizing about, and squeaked when Baron grabbed her arm and pulled her around to face the workout equipment. Gunner was sitting on a short bench with a…was that a paddle in his hand?

She planned a quick exit from the room, but got nowhere since Baron still had a hold of her arm.

"Come on, Stretch, your mouth is usually running with insults, so we decided to give you a reason to call us names. Gunner has something to give you, and I have to say, I'm planning to watch and enjoy every minute of it."

He towed her to what she'd thought was a pommel horse, but was actually just a wide padded beam, and pushed her over the thing, almost sending her onto her head. She tried to rise back up but he was in front of her securing her wrists to the legs of the contraption. She was afraid and excited all at once, but refused to give into his domination easily. Gunner had one of her ankles in his hand and hooked her leg up to her knee through a leather sling that was wrapped around the padded beam. She fought his strength when he pulled the other leg up.

"When I saw your legs split as if you didn't have bones hooking them together like you did, I wanted to do this, so since I'm a selfish son-of-a-bitch, we're doing this my way. I can see those hoops in your nipples too. Baron, did you see those?" Gunner ran his big hands wide across her thighs, and onto the generous mounds of the cheeks of her ass. He squeezed the globes in his hands and groaned. "This is a goddamned work of art. Come on over here, man, you gotta see this."

Baron was busy himself and told him so. "I'll get there, right now I'm having some fun with these tits. Do you want the clamp on her clit? Or should I use two of these clamps on her lips?"

Gunner leaned down and considered the question, "How about just clamping the nipples and hanging a weight from them. That way the clamps won't get in the way when I slap this pussy." She made a few short squeals of distress when Baron clamped each nipple, but wasn't protesting what they were doing. That fact wasn't unobserved by either man.

When Gunner tested her reactions with several sharp swats on her ass, and a good slap directly over her clit, he had all the answers he needed. He bent down again to look into her red face. "Oh, baby, you should have told us that you like our brand of play. Your pussy just pushed out enough juice to lube all of us and have more to play with later. It's no wonder you're being such a nasty mouthed bitch. Frustration makes women evil." Baron's fingers were already dragging fingers soaked in her juices from the other side of the beam, and painting her tiny wrinkled hole.

Gunner kept watch to see what her reaction to that was. Her eyes widened and her mouth opened, and he thought she was going to say something, but she squeezed those baby blues and scrunched her mouth shut. So, they could safely believe that she hadn't been fucked in the ass before, or if she had, it wasn't a happy memory. "You just stay there, and we'll enjoy giving you what you need. If you whimper and cry enough, Baron might even be nice and crack that asshole of yours wide open with an anchor to give you a little extra before one of us fuck you there." He saw her shiver and that was good enough for him. He stepped away to open the cabinet on the wall.

He heard a sharp cry and glanced over his shoulder to see Baron was slowly pushing two fingers into her back entrance, it didn't surprise him in the least to see the stainless steel set of graduating sized anchors balanced on the beam next to her thigh. He turned back to the task at hand and chose a rat tailed whip. The handle was short, but there was plenty of flexible leather to give her what she needed. The paddle he'd originally held before was not the kind that he wanted to test her needy ass out on. Her gasping scream gave him a reason to hurry back to watch Baron penetrating her tight hole with a medium sized metal cylinder. The deeper he pushed it in, the more she squealed.

Baron was fascinated with the sight of the cold metal stretching her dainty asshole. Damn but he could hardly hold himself back from removing the thing entirely and shoving his hard cock as deep as it would go. He took it slowly, giving her an inch at a time, pulling it out and sliding it back in further each time until it was seated the entire four inches available. He rubbed the cheeks of her ass and watched them quiver when he removed his hands. He bent down and saw that her eyes were closed and her jaw was clenching. "Look at me." Her eyes remained closed. "I said look at me." He tapped the clips on her breasts and got her to open her eyes, and he could see that she was fine. Her eyes all but rolled back in her head when he twisted the clamps. "It looks as if we found the right woman to play with tonight, didn't we?"

He sat down on his ass and scooted forward until his hard cock was within licking distance of her lips. "I'm going to let you lick my cock, but don't take it into your mouth yet. Gunner just picked out a nice whip to stripe your disrespectful ass with, and I want to see you enjoy it without too many distractions." He twisted the clamps again, a bit further this time and she cried out, but didn't object. "You can tell me if we get too rough you know. It's been a long time since we had a playmate that likes to feel the bite of pain with her pleasure. Now I'm taking my cock out of my jeans, and you're going to lick, remember? No, nodding won't do it, Stretch, I want the words, do you understand?"

She gasped, "Yes," at the same time she felt the first sting of the whip. She was afraid to speak because she was afraid she would ask them to spank her and use her in any way they wanted to. From the minute Baron had grabbed her arm and began bending her over the beam, she wanted this. Before she left the shower, she'd fantasized about them taking her the way she yearned for a man to take her, and now the two men were fulfilling her dream, and she didn't want them to stop. The excitement of being bound over this contraption, and being spanked shifted her sexual needs into overdrive.

When Baron shimmied out of his jeans, shucking them down to his ankles, she didn't bother to try to tease him about going commando, the rhythmic sting of the whip on her cheeks and thighs made her scream in gratitude for giving her what she wanted. Baron's monster cock would fill her mouth and stretch her lips wide, if he decided to allow her to suck him off. His size was a surprise, she'd been expecting well-endowed, but this went above and beyond her expectations. He watched her curl her tongue around the underside of the head, and watched as her tongue bathed him with warm moisture. She gathered the pre-cum from his tip and swallowed it with a moan. Every touch, every swat with the whip and Gunner's large punishing hand gave her pleasure, she felt alive and greedily hoped they would keep it up until none of them could walk.

The metal anchor in her butt felt foreign at first. She had allowed Arlan to try fucking her ass once. Since neither of them had tried backdoor sex before, it had turned into a disaster. Baron had claimed that he would be fucking her ass later, and from the size of his cock, she knew it would hurt, and still she wanted it. She wanted everything the two men had to offer, and she planned to take it. Tomorrow she could reclaim her independence and control of her life. Tonight she was going to be the masochist that enjoyed pain filled pleasure. The sharp slaps to her wet pussy stung, but she felt her orgasm building fast and hoped for more of the unusual stimulation. She whispered, "More please." Gunner couldn't possibly have heard her, but he continued to spank her wet flesh, and she fell into the most powerful orgasm she'd ever enjoyed. She screamed and tried to pump her hips. Her hands grabbed onto the thick wood they were bound to and she wanted more. On her last yell, Baron pushed his cock straight up and into her mouth. She took him as deep as she could, ignoring her gag reflex as much as possible, and swallowing back the bile attempting to come from her stomach.

Gunner pulled the metal toy from her rear hole and watched as the hole stayed open for a moment before it again became a tiny spiral of wrinkled flesh. He bent and gave the little spot a lick, and decided to replace the one he removed with the larger one. If she was going to have both him and Baron fucking her holes tonight, she would need to be as open as possible before hand. He used the lube in the box to make sure there would be an easy slide when he pushed the thick metal inside her ass. Watching it widen her hole until the delicate flesh was stretched as wide as the anchor was thick gave him a pang that Baron would be the one to crack this particular half broken in cherry. He wanted to sink his prick deep and let her body squeeze the come from his balls through his cock. He worked the metal as deep as he could and was tickled to hear her sharp scream. He looked down and saw that Baron was watching him fuck her with the anchor.

Baron scooted backwards on his ass until he could reach his boots to remove them and his jeans from his ankles. Afterwards, he untied the restraints holding Amy's wrists to the posts, and stood up. "Oh, brother, would you look at that, those stripes are beautiful, man, you did good. She's loving it all. She went after my cock like she was starved to death. I bet her pussy is dying for a bit of attention though. When you spanked it, she went off big time. Let's take her to the bedroom, or pull one of the mats over here and give her something to really scream about."

# CHAPTER EIGHT

They ended up on the wrestling mat on the floor. Amy was thankful they let her legs loose, she was developing a cramp in her thigh muscle that was distracting her from enjoying the things they were doing to her body. When her legs were planted on the floor again, she felt the thing in her butt readjust, and almost came from the stinging burn caused by the toy. She grabbed onto the beam and bent slightly, dropping her head and breathing through her nostrils. The deep trembles calmed a bit, but she knew every small step would stimulate those nerves that were already screaming at her from being stretched.

She wanted them. One would do the trick to satisfy the empty feeling in her pussy, but the two of them would finish her off. *What a way to go, I can deal with that*. The clamps on her nipples had long since turned the nubbins numb, but each shuddering breath she took caused them to pull just a little to remind her they were there. She looked under her arm to see what the men were doing, and saw Gunner finish removing his jeans. Baron was out of her view, but she knew he was there somewhere.

She tried to straighten her body so she could walk, but that wasn't happening in her present condition. She was going to come right where she stood, and she grabbed the beam harder, as she rode out the small but powerful tremors causing her to cry out, and land on her knees. She spied Gunner sitting comfortably on his ass on a grey padded mat, and began crawling to him. She would take his cock into her pussy and ride him until he cried for mercy. She felt wild and ready to take what she wanted, fuck them, they were prey.

He was smiling as she crawled in a direct line toward where he sat. She would teach him to smile like that. He would beg and she would fuck him, then she would fuck his buddy too. She kept her eye on the hard pole sticking up from the thick patch of hair at his crotch. It was as impressive as Baron's prick was, but she would soon show them impressive. A song began in her head and she smiled, her movements were timed to the music in her brain, and her hips swayed in a slow seductive rhythm until she got to Gunner. She lifted her leg and stretched it over his hips, and settled her center over his hard cock.

Gunner sat back and kept his upper body lifted by planting his elbows on the mat so he could watch her little pussy absorb his prick. Her hips rose and fell in small increments until he wanted to slam himself as deep as he could. When he put his hands on her hips to shove her down over him, she snarled at him and sank her nails into his belly.

"Move and I will gut you, just sit back, and leave me alone, this is my turn."

Baron laughed, but she ignored him. Gunner held up his hands to show her that she had free access. He was grinning, but his teeth were clenched. "Hey, man, you need to take that thing outta her ass, my prick is being—Oh fuck, yeah, like that, baby." She had finally seated herself on his cock, and sealed her wet lips to his hairy flesh. Her nails must be drawing blood about now, but he didn't give a shit. She could do anything she wanted as long as she kept that strange rhythm going.

She felt Baron behind her and wondered if he was going to take the toy from her ass. His cock was way too big to be inside of her at the same time Gunner was seated so deep. She felt his fingers pull at the metal, drawing it from her body. He pushed her torso down onto Gunner's chest and she latched onto the nipple closest to her lips. He grabbed her hair with both hands and directed her in harsh whispers between his clenched teeth. "Lick and suck, don't bite my fuckin' nipple off." She felt the slide of the toy slowly exiting her ass and began to pant.

Baron watched the way her asshole clenched on the shiny anchor. He could hardly wait to bury his cock as deep as he could go. He tossed the toy aside and lubed his hard prick liberally. He liked the thin lube, it wasn't the thick greasy stuff that he'd used for years until he found this stuff. He held himself at the entrance to her little hole, anticipating the heat and tight muscles that would glove him tighter than any pussy ever could. He loved being the first to crack a woman's asshole like this. His prick was looking forward to the experience too, if the pre-cum coming from its tip was any indication.

"She's gonna feel this, buddy. It's going to be a tight fit," he warned Gunner because she would be screaming as soon as the thick head of his cock pushed through her ringed muscle.

Gunner tried to lift her from his prick. If Baron was going in hot, she would be stuffed with cock, and the two of them were more than enough to fuck her up bad if they weren't careful. "Let up, Baron is about to stuff your backdoor and it's going to hurt for a few minutes until you get used to him being in there. Come on, let up on my prick, I'll give it back to you as soon as I can."

She bared her teeth at him and tried to stay seated, but he pulled back and lifted her with his hands until he was out of her wet heat, and was resting under her soaked clit and lips. He watched her face to gauge her response to the invasion into her smallest entrance. He could feel the pressure Baron's cock was causing, and saw her mouth open in a short cry. She began panting again, and sucking in air, only to blow it out through her pursed lips. That tactic of coping with having Baron's cock steadily pushing forward gave way to a low toned teeth gritting scream. Gunner decided to help her by pulling the clamps on her nipples and twisting them. She looked down to his face and he released the clamps completely, both at the same time. She drew back, almost shoving her body away from his fingers. Her eyes flew open even wider as she realized she'd just shoved her ass completely over the thick cock inside. She screamed, and Baron yelled at the sensation of her tight asshole squeezing his prick in her distress.

He tried to stay as still as possible, enjoying the way her muscles relaxed and clenched in turn. He wasn't going to last more than a stroke or two this time around. He heard Gunner asking her if she was dealing, and she nodded her head. She began to move slightly, and each time she moved she gasped, and he knew she was trying to adjust. She pulled up a few inches, breathing like she'd been running, and slid back down onto him. "That's right, Stretch, you take your time and take what you need. I'm not going anywhere; your ass is so tight I'm going to try to wait for you to find your happy spot." He hoped she would find it pretty damn quick, or she would be humping on his deflating cock.

He could feel Gunner underneath them and knew that their balls were up close and personal, it wasn't the first time and wouldn't be the last that it happened. The first few times he'd felt Gunner's cock sliding through the other side of that thin tissue between a woman's asshole and pussy, he almost freaked out. The feeling of a tight hole and the massage the men shared by moving their cocks, was indescribable. He didn't want to kiss Gunner, or anything else he associated with gay sex, but the slide inside a woman, and the bump and grind was damn near addictive. Their balls were usually hanging around and bumping into each other at some point during a ménage, and it no longer gave him the weirds, now he accepted the sensation as another touch of enjoyment. The two of them had talked about the whole men on men thing and decided that this was the only way they felt comfortable touching each other. It worked for them, and his thoughts hadn't been distracting enough to calm his come from boiling up ready to hose her ass full of sperm. She was sliding up and down on him easier now and she was screaming again, he felt the clench of her orgasm take hold of her and he let his own pleasure take him right along with hers.

Gunner had felt the lips and her inner flesh begin to spasm, and he didn't bother to hold back. Her cunt was gliding back and forth over him, smashing his prick between his own body and hers. The stimulation was too much for him to ignore, and he shot his load between them. He held her jaws with his hands and wiped her tears with his thumbs, as the clear liquid fell from her glazed eyes. She was still shuddering, and he felt Baron leave her body, so he flipped her onto her back and kept his thigh between her open legs. "That was fucking beautiful, baby. Now I want you to give me one more thing, do you think you can stay with me for a minute or two?" She might have nodded, he was busily wetting his first two fingers in their sticky combined juices. He knew she would love this as much as he would.

He slipped his soaked fingers up into her tunnel and groaned at the small tremors he could feel that were keeping her from complete satisfaction. He hooked his fingers up and pulled hard. He let the pressure up a bit and began to rub the small patch of her G-spot. "Come on, baby, you can let it go, you're going to squirt just like we do, I know it's there, just waiting, come on, you're not gonna piss yourself, it's just your pussy squirting, let it go, babe. I'm right here to catch you."

Baron sat by her head and hoisted her head and shoulders onto his thighs. His big hands were playing with her breasts, and when she gasped at the sensations Gunner's fingers were causing, Baron squeezed her nipples hard. She felt the liquid shoot from her body and kept curling her body with the need to bear down. Gunner grinned and nodded at her, telling her, "Oh fuck, baby, look at that, did that feel as good as it looked like it did? I love to see a woman shoot like that. It takes a special pussy to be able to let herself enjoy this kind of orgasm. I'm so fuckin' proud of you." He leaned in and kissed her on the clit, while Baron fucked her mouth with his.

*****

Baron was the first of them to stir from his head on her breast. "Come on, Stretch, let's get cleaned up, and find the bed." He got to his feet with a deep groan and looked at the scratches he'd gained while she was enjoying that last orgasm. His forearms were sporting a few nice nail trails where she had grabbed on to ride it out. He reached down and pulled her to her feet, and he bent down to pick her up to carry her to the shower. She didn't offer any resistance, and that was a good thing, he was tired, and tomorrow was going to be a bitch if he didn't get at least a few hours of sleep. Gunner was almost asleep where he was laying, but Baron wasn't worried about him. He would eventually rise and clean up before getting some sleep himself.

He took Amy to the shower and stood her against the wall while he lathered up his hands and washed every inch of her. She blushed when his hands touched between her ass cheeks, but he let it pass without commenting. Both of them were ready to drop from exhaustion, and he wrapped her in a towel to take her to his bed.

Melvin was pissed at him because Baron had locked him in the bedroom while the humans were in the playroom. There was pillow stuffing all over the room and on the bed from his tantrum. "You little son-of-a-bitch, you ripped my fucking pillow into a goddamned mess. That's it, tomorrow I buy a crate for your ass to go into when I want some privacy."

Amy was giggling and trying to brush the fluffy pillow stuffing off the bed. She pulled the top cover off the bed and crawled between the sheets. Melvin ran around to the opposite side of the bed, and took a running leap to land on her side of the big bed. He hunkered down in the curve of her waist and hip, tucked his head down, so the pissed off man wouldn't see him, after all, if he couldn't see Baron, then Baron couldn't see him.

*****

Gunner woke feeling cold and remembered where he was when he rolled to his side onto the cold spot next to him. He got to his feet and wiped a hand down his face. The room wasn't much of a mess, but he hated leaving the equipment out and used without cleaning the items and putting them away. He gathered the box of metal anchors, which were little more than glorified metal butt plugs. They did the job, but they weren't what they'd been advertised as either. He hoped he would remember that fact when he helped Baron do the ordering for the sex shop next time. One good thing about owning a sex shop, they could actually recommend items they'd used and liked. It was one of the great perks for owning a business that was picketed every few months by the Bible Thumpers that wore their religion in daylight hours, and snuck into the shop after dark to purchase everything from sex manuals, to full out hardcore foot long dildos and leather whips.

He washed the metal plugs and dried them before placing them back in the box and putting them away. The restraints they'd used were in good shape and he put them aside to oil later. The whip he'd used was fine and good to stripe her ass again. He put everything neatly away and wiped down the padded beam and mat. When everything was back to order, he went into the shower and washed the scent of Amy's sex from his flesh. He had to take his cock in hand and wring its neck, because thoughts of watching her crawl over him, daring him to stop her from sliding her pink flesh over his and demanding he let her take him her way made his prick hard. He was an equal opportunity fucker. If she liked riding, he was down with that occasionally. He shot his load down the drain with the soap bubbles and rinsed off.

# CHAPTER NINE

Amy came awake with a heavy weight lying over her ankles. She was on her stomach, and drool was still wet on her cheek when she turned her head to see what was holding her legs down. Melvin was staring at her with his tongue hanging from the side of his mouth, and when he saw her watching him, he stood and stretched. She rolled over and looked at her surroundings. There was still fluffy pillow stuffing all over the room. That probably explained Melvin's presence. If she remembered correctly, Melvin was under a dog crate sentence for his hissy fit, and staying out of sight.

She realized that she was naked under the sheet, and wondered if she could pilfer a t-shirt or something to cover her bare body. She went to the only other piece of furniture in the room. The lowboy had a mirror that was dusty and looked like it was never cleaned. She avoided looking at her reflection, knowing that her hair would be a tangled mess. She was a bit sore in spots that had been forgotten over time, and had to smile when she remembered last night's activities. Well, the good parts of the evening after they'd come here to Baron's home anyway.

She opened the top two drawers and found several pairs of jeans and sweats. The small drawer held men's boxers, most of them still had the tags on them. She chose a dark green pair, and found a drawer stuffed full of t-shirts. The first one had the typical picture of a pig sitting back on the seat of a

93

hog. The second shirt has a caricature of a naked woman with huge breasts that were barely covered with a string type of bikini. She ended up taking a white wife beater that appeared to be way too small for either man. It was new, and she was happy that she'd found something to cover her naked body.

She explored the house on her way to the kitchen, why the man had four bedrooms, she had no idea. Two of the rooms were empty, and there was a guest bath between the rooms, with a door leading into each bedroom. Counting the master bath, there were three full baths, not counting the one in the basement. So much for the dirty, greasy biker persona, she had found his kryptonite. He had a thing for bathrooms. The knowledge made her giggle. He probably had a perfectly good reason for having a four bedroom, four bath house in the middle of a forested front yard, and a beautiful yard in the back. This place should have been filled with screaming kids and laundry hanging on a line in the sunshine.

The kitchen was large with long countertops and modern appliances. Looking around the house, she could see there was a bare minimum of furnishings, and the place could use a serious cleaning. The kitchen had a toaster and coffee maker on the counter, along with a bag of dog kibble and an overflowing trash can. She checked the fridge and found a half gallon of milk, two green hairy bagels, and an egg carton with two eggs inside. Two shelves of the space were filled with beer, and a bottle of whiskey. The freezer held four cardboard pizzas, ice cubes, a box of popsicles, and toaster pastries. Melvin left her by way of his own door, presumably to take care of his doggy duties.

The coffee in the pot was cold and rank, so she rinsed out the pot and brewed a new one. She helped herself to the toaster pastries and enjoyed the sweet breakfast while looking out into the backyard. The squirrels and rabbits didn't seem to worry about Melvin as he sniffed out his favorite spots.

The sink load of plastic forks and plates took her a half an hour to wash and dry. Since the cupboards were practically empty of serving ware, she stuck the clean items in the cupboard closest to the sink, and looked around for something new to do. It didn't surprise her that she had been left behind when the men left this morning, in fact she hadn't even heard them leave. Her peek out of the kitchen window into the carport, showed the bikes were gone, so she assumed they must have left very early, since it was eight thirty now.

By noon, she had dusted, swept the bedroom, bathrooms, and kitchen. She was saving the hardwood floors to do in the afternoon. Melvin kept her company by following her around and lying on the floor surfaces that she'd just swept. She figured he was marking his territory without hiking his leg or peeing on anything in the house. Her purse was missing, and with that so was her phone, leaving her no means of communicating with anyone if she had a friend to call anyway. She watched the talk show host telling a couple that they were lousy parents, and she had to agree with his assessment. The parents were lousy. Their four children lived with the grandparents and were divided between the two families, shuttled between them in turns on opposite weeks. It was so depressing she cried along with the six year old that didn't understand why mommy and daddy didn't want her and her siblings. *Because they are selfish bastards that only want to have a good time, their poor old parents don't need to have a retirement and decent life as they grow old, hell no, they can raise your lazy ass's kids.* She turned the TV off and got to work on the floors.

At four, she was as done as she could get, given the lack of cleaning supplies and the last load of bedding was in the dryer. There was a stack of men's t-shirts and jeans on the dresser, and the towels had been put away in the hall closet. The whore's bath she'd taken to rinse off the sweat from her labors had rejuvenated her and she wanted to explore outside, but the only foot protection she had were those fuck me boots and they weren't designed to walk around in grass and dirt in.

She swiped a pillow from the only other bedroom that had a bed, to replace the one that Melvin took apart last night, and the little beast appeared to be grinning as she slipped a clean pillowcase over it. "If you rip another pillow up I am not going to clean the mess, Melvin, you were a bad boy." He didn't seem to be upset that she was threatening him. In fact, he barked and headed for the kitchen, ran through his door and took off down the driveway.

Within minutes, she heard the rumble of a motorcycle, and knew he must have heard Baron pulling into the driveway. She watched as the bike pulled into the carport, and the biker dismounted. It wasn't Baron. In fact she had never seen this man before. He was an older man with a long grey ponytail, wraparound shades, and he appeared to be one walking mass of tattoos. He walked around outside of the house, and she was scared shitless that he would break in. She couldn't call the cops, she couldn't call Baron or Gunner. If he decided to come inside to steal something, she was a sitting duck. When he walked back into the carport, she ran into Baron's bedroom and yanked the long sleeved denim jacket from the inside of the closet where she'd put it earlier. She tried to be as quiet as possible when she raised the window and pushed the screen out. She heard breaking glass, and stopped trying to be delicate. Her ass was through the window and she was pulling it back down as low as she could from the outside, so he wouldn't know she'd left from the room. Hopefully, he would have no idea that someone had been in the house. She ran for the trees and tried to keep as low as possible. He must not have clued in on her presence, because there had been no bullets or running feet chasing her. Her feet were paying the price for the lack of footwear, but adrenalin kept her from stopping to nurse them. Until she got deep enough into the woods to hide, she would keep moving.

The scent of smoke filled the air and she heard the roar of several other bikes coming from behind her at the house. She sat behind a thick trunked tree and tried to catch her breath.

*****

Baron saw Melvin on the side of the road. He'd just started to pull into the driveway at the club when he spied the little dog lying on his belly three feet off the pavement. *What the fuck*? Melvin had been left with Stretch, back at the house. Someone must have gone over there and brought her back here. Someone was going to get their asses kicked. Why poor Mel was outside of the compound was another mystery. If one of those dumb fucks had let him out of the gate, they would be paying with their front teeth.

Melvin was breathing, but the little guy couldn't stand worth a shit. Baron picked him up and set him between his thighs for the ride into the club's grounds. He parked his bike and carried Mel inside. His boot kicked the door open, and he started yelling. "I want the motherfucker that left Melvin outside of the gates, and I want his ass in front of me fucking now." Several heads turned his way, but no one volunteered themselves to know anything either.

Myrtle looked at Melvin and rushed around from behind the bar. "Where did you find him? As far as I know, no one has been here most of the day, not since this morning when a greybeard Nomad came through here by the name of Bruin. I've never seen him before, but he wears a cut covered in patches. One of them was an original, and I noticed a 1%. He has more tats than most of the guys here together, and drives a fatboy. He is one scary bastard, Baron. His eyes are dead, you know what I mean? Everybody is at the day jobs or sleeping before noon, you know that." She took Melvin behind the bar and set a dish of water down by his muzzle. It didn't take much to get him to drink. She had to take the water away when he lapped up almost half of it without stopping.

"He wanted to know who the new Prez is, and where to find you. I gave him your cell number, he sucked some suds, and left within the hour, I'd say it was close to noon."

He had no idea who the brother was. Nomads were usually younger than a man the age that Myrtle was describing. And an original 1% was hard to find still roaming without a companion and a feeding tube. If he was from the mother club in Ohio, that might explain it. Those men were flat out road warriors. They were tough bastards that believed in the club, and not much else. His old man had been an original, and so was Gunner's dad. He'd met Beast twice, and if the man wasn't doing life in San Quentin, Myrtle could have been describing him. Fuck it, he wanted to make sure Mel was all right, and collect Stretch. He'd been thinking about that soft skin all day and wanted to taste her this time. Gunner was supposed to be bringing food to the crib, and they planned to have a heart to heart with their houseguest.

"Where's Amy? I left her and Mel at the house this morning." He didn't like the look of confusion that he was seeing on Myrtle's face. "What?"

"I have been here all day, Amy isn't here."

He stood still for minute to take in what she was saying. Melvin lifted his head and gave him a tired look. The little fucker had run what, five miles to get help? Telling himself to hang on, this isn't some damn Lassie episode, did no good. The more he stared at Melvin and looked at his paws, the more convinced he became. He'd left Amy alone, with no phone, and no wheels, thinking she wouldn't be able to do something stupid, like go back to her apartment. *Fuck.*

He saw Leech and Preacher playing poker with those two knuckleheads, Gator and Barney. "Mount up, ladies, it looks like we're going dancing." He bent down to give Mel a scratch on his head. "You did good, Mel."

He walked out the door with the four men on his heels. Burger decided he needed to take a ride, and kicked the chair Skids was sleeping in. "Let's go, Baron has a party going, we won't want to miss that."

*****

Bruin watched the kid that was supposed to be his pride and joy, sucking on a fuckin' crack pipe, while his handler, Reeker, sat next to him trying to convince him that the new Prez named Baron was jealous and unfairly stripped him of his place in the Breed.

Bruin had been through the house, and the pole barn. He didn't see as much as a roach, let alone any evidence the man was manufacturing Meth and had intentionally hooked his son on the stuff. The call from David's mother telling him the boy needed help, and that he was totally out of control, even to the point of saying her daughter was in danger from the boy and the men he was with. That was some messed up shit. She was right about one thing. The company he was keeping was dogshit.

He hadn't decided whether to kill the kid or not, but the fucker that he called his President, Reeker, was John Doe.

They were sitting in the backyard at Baron's place. Bruin told the seven scrawny followers of John Doe, to keep their asses outside, and he stayed with them. When this Baron got home, they were going to sit down and have a talk.

They had built a small bonfire in the metal ring between the pole barn and the house. When Baron came home, there would be no hiding. Reeker was the only one that tried to hide and ambush the owner, but Bruin warned him that he would frown on such chicken shit action. "Are you a man, or a fuckin' split tail? You want me to take out this guy, but you want to pussy up and hide? I ain't no fuckin' coward, and I won't line up with anybody that is. You got seven, drug addicted, snot nosed kids that couldn't find their dicks with both fucking hands, and you. What's to be afraid of?"

He got sick of watching his kid sucking on that damn pipe like it was a mother's titty, and stood up. He walked over to David and knocked the glass cylinder out of the boy's skinny fingers. The kid was dumb enough to call him a name and got laid out for his troubles. He hadn't hit him very hard, but it was enough to knock the boy out. He left him where he laid, disgusted with the situation. He walked over to the closest tree and took a leak.

He turned around and saw Reeker heading for the bikes. Yeah, he was a rat. His aim was true. He hoped Baron had a place nice and obscure to deposit John Doe. He was contemplating just taking out all of the fuckers, and leaving them for the Prez as a gift, while he wiped the blade off on the candy ass's t-shirt. Unfortunately, David was his only kid. He didn't love the kid, didn't even like him. He wasn't around while the kid grew up, and until his mother called all over hell and back looking for him, he had no idea the boy tried to follow his path. The kid was spoiled, and now he was trying to stay a kid without responsibility, even for himself. From the look of him, he would be dead without intervention within a short period of time anyway. The boy was nothing but skin over bones, with sunken eyes and sores speckling his face. He was driving a piece of shit rat bike with bald fucking tires and no lights.

If he allowed the kid to live, it was going to be a long fucking road to hoe. David would be a bloody mess by the time he was detoxed off the fuckin poison in his body. The boy needed food and sleep. Not more shit frying his damn brain. Bruin knew what he was talking about when it came to addiction. He'd gotten his speed on in Nam, graduated to heroin and LSD, it took two stints in the cage to clean him up. Now he smoked a little weed to wind down, and stuck to beer for his buzz.

He was one of the original Lucifer's Breed. There had been ten of them. Now there was three left above ground. He was a lucky son-of-a-bitch to have such a legacy to leave behind and he felt pride every time he saw their logo. Maybe he would give the kid some instruction for a while, see if he would straighten his shit out. If not, there was always the other option. He heard the rumble of several bikes, and sat his ass on a log, hands visible, clasped together between his spread thighs. He wasn't going to defend this pack of jackals, except for David, for him, he would negotiate.

# CHAPTER TEN

Baron rode in front of the pack. He didn't ever show weakness to anyone. If this Bruin was a threat, he would take care of him. His brain wanted to see Amy, but he had to access the situation first. It looked like they'd made themselves at home, but why were they outside? Something wasn't right here. He pulled into the carport. It was his fucking place. The fatboy was flat black and a painted capitol O with #1 under it was on the top of the gas tank.

The men who followed him from the club were already surrounding the pack of starved looking walking skeletons that were scared shitless, but were trying to act tough. One of them was on the ground out cold. He walked toward the man sitting by the fire and noticed Leech rolling a body over with his foot. Baron looked back to the greybeard and wondered what the old boy was playing at.

Bruin liked the way this new Prez held himself, the man's eyes gave nothing away. Even when he saw the John Doe lying on the ground, there was no emotion. He was a big motherfucker for sure, his posse knew what their role was, and it looked like they trusted him to do his.

"Thanks for taking out the trash, but I don't think I've had the pleasure." Baron held out his hand to the man. He wasn't surprised when Bruin stood and clasped his hand. The old guy had dignity, he could respect that, but if he'd come here for something more than what could be seen on the surface, now would be a good time to say so. "We good here? Or do we have business to discuss?"

Right to the point, he was beginning to wish this guy was his kid instead of the rack of drugged out bones still laid out on the grass. "Tags Bruin, out of the mother chapter. I didn't come here to bust your balls, I'm here because I got a message from the mother of my son telling me the boy was having problems. I show up and he's with John Doe who's feeding him street drugs and talking shit. That's him over there where I made him take a nap. As soon as he wakes up, I'll be taking him off your hands. A boy should have a man to influence him, and so far I have been pretty busy, I plan to take some time to remedy his lack of education.

"By the way, I had an accident with your window, and I might have wandered around looking for someone to talk to."

Baron nodded his head acknowledging the man's admitted home invasion. He wondered how Amy took that. She was probably scared to death. "How did my house guest take your tour?" He was getting real tired of seeing that confused look on peoples' faces when Amy was mentioned. "Is she hiding in a closet?"

The reply was not what he expected. Bruin's denial of meeting Amy was the truth, he could see it, so where did she go?

"I didn't see anyone here, and I think she might have made enough noise to let me know if she was in a closet. The doors I opened did sound like someone was behind them, but it turned out that your mice are noisy. Might want to get a cat."

What the hell? She didn't even have a set of clothes other than what she'd walked in the place with last night, and, fuck. What the hell was she up to. "Come on inside, I need a beer, and I guess I need to look around some myself."

As the two men walked toward the house, they could hear Burger telling their prisoners they needed to shut the fuck up or something bad was going to happen. "You little bitch boys should have stayed home living in your grandma's basement. Give us any trouble and we'll make sure your grandparents won't have to worry about you ever again." Baron smiled.

"That's Burger, he can be a mean son-of-a-bitch."

Leech had Gator cleaning up the glass on the kitchen floor when they walked into the carport. While they waited for him to finish, they discussed the merits of the comfortable road bike that Bruin drove. "I just acquired her about a year ago, gotta say she's a nice smooth ride. My old bones don't creak nearly as bad as they used to after a long haul, and if I'm in a hurry, the extra fuel in the tanks keep me going a few more miles down the road before I have to stop."

Baron nodded and kept up his side of the conversation, but his concern for Amy was growing. She should have come out of hiding when Leech and Preacher went through the house. He handed Bruin a beer, took one for himself, and excused himself for a few minutes. Leech sat with the greybeard and began to talk. He would guarantee that by the time he was finished with the conversation, the two men would be friendly. Leech was the people person in the group, and he had no problem when it came to talking to perfect strangers.

He searched the entire house, including the attic and under the beds for Amy, she wasn't there. It started raining and he could hear thunder in the distance, so he closed the windows in each room he searched. He'd shut the window in his room thinking it was strange the screen had fallen out, that's when he realized he was a dumbass.

She must have climbed out of the window when company arrived. He hurried back through the house and out the sliding door leading onto the deck. There was a man hiding under the deck looking scared and when Baron saw him, he yelled to Burger. "Got a rabbit here, under the deck." He kept heading around the side of the house. Preacher and Barney followed to see what was happening.

The screen was lying under the window. That was all they found to show where she'd exited the house. Baron looked around, and the only cover on this side of the house was the woods. They headed for the trees, and he told them he thought Amy was hiding there somewhere. The rain was coming down harder, and it was cold. Fall was beginning early this year, so he hoped they would find her before too much longer. After dark the temps dropped pretty low, even in this part of the country. The wind was picking up and lightning began to slice through the early evening sky. They'd gone a good five hundred feet into the woods and waded through brush to their knees, when he spotted something white about twenty yards ahead.

When he drew nearer, he was happy to have found her. He shouted to the others over the howling wind, and hurried to see if she was hurt. She was covered in scrapes and it appeared she was allergic to some vegetation, if the red rash he saw on her arms was any indication of her condition. She was shivering so bad her teeth were chattering, as she huddled in his denim jacket, with her arms wrapped around her bare legs. She was bare footed, but she was alive and he gathered her into his arms making shushing noises for her benefit.

"Come on, Stretch, let's get you to the house, and warm you up. I'll call Doc and get him over here to check you out. That was smart of you to slip out of the window like you did. I almost didn't notice the screen was missing." He pulled her upright, but knew she wouldn't be able to walk back through the woods and briars. Her legs were a mass of scratches, some of them looked pretty deep, and her feet were caked with blood soaked mud on the toes and soles. He pulled her into his arms and told her to wrap her legs around his waist. "I'm going to carry you out of here, but you need to hold on to me, and don't strangle me or we'll never get you warm and dry."

She told him what happened on the walk back. He'd had to put her down twice to climb over a couple of downed trees, and he'd stumbled once when his boot slid in the mud, but they finally made it to the edge of the woods, near the house. Gunner and Zippy were headed their way. When they reached the spot that Baron stopped and stood Amy on her feet to rest his back and neck, Gunner took over carrying her to the house. The rain was relentless, and he slid through the soaked grass, but held her as close as he could. Baron followed them inside.

Baron changed clothes quickly, leaving Amy with Gunner, knowing she would be taken care of. The storm wasn't letting up, but he still had to see to the rest of the people at the house. He was happy to see Gunner, Zippy, and Chaucer had brought a few bags of eats. They were going to have to do until someone could go out for more.

Bruin dragged his boy into the carport and tossed a silver blanket over his shivering body after he pulled a roll of duct tape from his saddlebags and taped the kid's ankles and hands together. When a gentle tap in the mouth didn't faze his son, he added a strip of the tape over his mouth. "Boy, I'm debating if you're worth the trouble it's gonna take to deal with you. Your best bet is to shut the fuck up, and sit your ass where I put you. You don't talk to an elder like that, and you damn sure better not talk to me that way again. You ain't pretty now, but you're gonna look kinda funny with no fuckin' teeth, you feel me?" David took his time, but he nodded his head.

He helped secure the rest of the troublemakers by using his roll of tape to keep them from roaming around. He found that Burger was a mean son-of-a-bitch when the dumbasses started to feel their high leaving and begged for a hit of anything to keep them from facing reality. He laughed at them, taunted them, and even shared a joint with Bruin, while they watched with hungry eyes.

Burger grinned when he announced he was going to request the Prez let him keep the men as pets. "I can leash them and chain them to a fuckin' post. They should be happy I'm thinking about keeping them, these little fuckers are givin' legitimate riders a bad name. All this random shit isn't what we do. If you're gonna fight, fight like a man, not some hidey-hole cocksucker. Men don't terrorize women, we fuck them. If they don't like it, we move on to the next one that will."

He looked at Bruin. "Wha'dya say, you wanna help me start a school to teach these sons-a-bitches manners and manhood?" From the horrified looks in the eyes of the captives that were coming down from their highs, both men laughed. "Or we can just kill them and put everyone out of their misery." Each time the thunder boomed overhead, a few of the captives would jump, and the men watching found it hilarious.

Zippy brought out two cardboard pizzas, and the men devoured them in front of the hollow eyed zombies. Only one of them looked at the food with any interest, but he finally turned his head to stare at the rain pouring off the roof.

Bruin crouched by his son and asked him, "Are you gonna eat the food and keep your words behind your teeth? Or should I let you go hungry for the night until you can learn to talk like a goddamned man instead of a pussy boy?" He ripped the tape from the kid's mouth and waited for David to speak.

110

The pizza went to his mouth, but no words came out. Bruin nodded, "You're learning."

They left Barney and Zippy to watch the men and headed into the house to warm up and grab a beer.

*****

Gunner stripped Amy down to her bare skin and ignored the old sayings about staying out of a bath when it was storming. She was still shivering and the only way to get her warm fast was a tub of steaming water. He stripped his clothes off too and sat behind her in the tub. He washed her bloody legs and arms and even got her hair washed. "Hey, you did good, you know? Thing is, you worried the shit out of us. I got here and seen everyone, but you, I thought something bad happened. You were gone, Baron was out looking for you, and all these fuckers were sitting around with their thumbs up their asses. Reeker, well, no one has to worry about him anymore, he is out of the picture. The old guy with the fatboy, he seemed to think you would know him, he says he is your brother's father."

She turned around in Gunner's arms and looked at him to see if he was joking. "Are you serious? I never knew him, or if I met him, I must have been very young. I just found out about his dad being a biker a month ago. I wonder where he's been all this time. David could have used a man's influence around. Our mother is not what you could call a fine example of parenting. I hate to say this, because she is my mom, but I've seen more devotion from a dog for her pups than our mother to her children. Some women should never have kids, she's one of them.

111

It looks like neither one of us was lucky in the father department either. Mine was a deadbeat asshole, and his is an absent biker. To borrow your words, it's a fucked up situation."

When the tremors stopped wracking her body, Gunner stood her up and used the shower to rinse the soap from their bodies. "Let's go, I'll get you tucked into bed, and find something for that growling stomach of yours."

Amy gave him a drowsy smile. "It's a good thing there's plenty of hot water. This is the second time I needed it, remember, last night? Baron helped then and now, thank you for helping me, I might have stayed in the tub and slept if you hadn't joined me." She got a kiss for her words, and he pulled the blanket up under her chin.

The red rash was gone after the bath, so whatever caused it must have been washed away with the bath water. Gunner set the bowl of canned soup that he'd heated in the microwave next to the bed on the nightstand. She was asleep, and her mouth was barely open, but she was snoring a little, and he found that adorable. He laid another blanket over the bed because it was chilly in the room, and he didn't want her to catch a cold. He shucked his clothes and joined her under the covers. When he pulled her into his arms, her head fit perfectly on his shoulder. He smiled as he drifted to sleep.

*****

Baron went out to check on the prisoners. He didn't plan to keep them around for long. They were men who had never matured past middle school brainpower. Now that they'd lost their drug daddy, they would be hanging on the streets looking for a fix. He decided to put the problem to the brothers tomorrow at Church. They couldn't let them go until they knew if that fucker Reeker had shared club business. David and the other kid whose name he couldn't remember, had been prospecting with the club for a few months, and who knew what they had picked up. He hesitated to kill them all, disposal wasn't the problem, he'd bet most of these assholes had families that cared about them, even in the shape they were in. Too many unknowns for his comfort, so they'd sit on them until a viable plan came up.

Currently, Barney and Chaucer were playing a game to keep them all entertained. He'd seen it before, actually instigated the game at times himself. Tonight, he sat it out and watched. The prisoners were sat in a circle and Chaucer explained the rules to them.

"Me and Barney here, we're bored, so you shitasses get to be the entertainment. You boys see this here revolver?" He spun the cylinder. "It's my personal protection. All I gotta do is point and shoot, no messing with an enemy, just shoot him and get it over with. So I'm gonna put a bullet in this ol' .38 special, and we're gonna play a game of Russian roulette. Only you boys get to be the targets." He grinned at the freckle faced kid with a red Mohawk. He looked at Barney and laughed.

Barney had a beat up semi-auto in his hand. "Now that's some funny shit there, do you boys see what Barney wants to use? That's cheating, man. You need a revolver for this game." The red

Mohawk had tears leaking down his face. He taunted each man in the circle by staring at him and grinning real slow. "If you're gonna play the game, you need to follow the rules." He kept spinning the cylinder.

Barney came back from the row of bikes with a .45 ACP hammerless. He made a production of breaking the gun down and inserting a moon clip. He had the loads made especially for noise instead of damage for those times an aggressive dog came after his scooter. He didn't want to admit that he hated to kill dumb animals. Men, he had no issue with killing. Dogs were just trying to guard their territory, same as he'd do for his if he had any. He was gonna catch shit for having them, but fuck it.

# CHAPTER ELEVEN

Chaucer stood in front of a skinny guy with no front teeth and a black eye. The kid closed his eyes and started begging for his life. He'd already pissed himself, and his tormentor found his tears funny. "Ain't you the one that told Barney to go fuck himself? I think I'll save you for him." He stepped to the next man and pointed his gun farther down. He pressed the trigger and nothing but the snap of the hammer was heard. The guy looked at him, and Chaucer laughed. "You thought I was gonna kill you? Hell no, you can live a nice long life without a dick, it ain't like any woman's gonna want to fuck your scrawny ass anyway." He made his way around the circle taunting each of his victims and shaking his head when the gun dry fired.

Barney stepped into the circle and saw the relief on four of the seven men's faces. "Well fuck, man, do you even have a damn bullet in that thing?" Chaucer laughed and pulled the trigger. A loud boom sounded and his victim screamed, clutching his crotch with both hands. There was a collective sigh of relief from the group and Barney pointed his gun and fired off three shots, three other men cried out and screamed in pain, grabbing their dicks through the denim.

The two grinning men laughed their asses off. Baron commented, "Those fucking loads would have taken their scalps off if I'd have shot them in the head." The wads in the blanks had enough velocity to cause pain, even through the thick material. It was all good. No one died, and even the ones that pissed themselves cried tears of relief. The rabbit that Baron saw under the deck was screaming at Barney.

"What kind of a sick psycho are you? We're tied up and can't fight back."

Barney didn't miss a beat, he stepped over to the kid and pulled the knife from his boot. When he'd sliced through the tape, he pulled the guy to his feet. He grabbed the filthy shirt covering a scrawny chest and shook him like a rag. "Boy, you wanna fight? I'll be happy to let you take the first swing, but you'd better be prepared to have your ass handed to you." The kid nodded, and several groans were heard behind him.

The little bastard had guts. Baron looked closer at the kid. He was skinny, but he didn't act like the rest of them. He wasn't twitchy or sobbing. He looked healthier than the others too. Barney was ready to square off with the kid, and Baron saw the way the boy shook out his muscles, and balance on his toes, before taking a stance. "Hang on a minute, Barney, let's make this fight is nice and fair, after all we don't want to send the boy home in a bag without giving him a fair fight, right? Let's take it to the yard." Chaucer went inside to let the men that wanted to see the entertainment know the boy challenged Barney.

Barney was a sociopathic little rooster on his best days. He was smaller than most of the brothers and he tried to make up for his size in actions. He wanted to be the first to fight, the first to get laid, the first to kill. He wasn't quiet about his accomplishments at the club either. The brother liked to brag about what a big man he was. He was not the only one with sociopathic tendencies, but he was the most annoying about it.

It was still raining, and the ground was soaked. The floodlights showing the backyard were lit up and everyone had a good view of the men. When Baron stood under the roof over the deck, most of the men inside came out to join him. Bruin stood close and eyed the opponents. "Which one do you have money on?"

The younger man smiled and told him, "I didn't place a bet, but my money would be on the kid." He went out in the yard to tell the kid the rules. "He beats your ass, you are advised to stay down, if you don't, he might kill you. Now how about you tell me what your name is and where you're from so I know where to send you back?"

The kid grudgingly told him, "My name's Bobby Dee, I come from a spot in the road called Bono in Arkansas." Baron noticed the kid looked him in the eye when he talked to him, he also didn't slump while he was standing there. *Yes indeed, there's more to you than meets the eyes.*

"Okay, this is a man on man fight, no knives, or guns. Show us a good fight, boys, we're stuck with each other at least until morning. Some of us are bored and need more entertainment." He left them standing in the yard and climbed back onto the deck. "Anytime you girls are ready, do it."

Chaucer was yelling for his buddy and giving him tips, Zippy came over to Baron, and leaned close. "That kid is gonna wipe the grass with

Barney. Do you see how he balances himself? I saw my little sister in her self-defense class stand like that. Thinking I might have to pay the boy for whippin' Barney's ass, 'cause I sure would like to see it happen."

Burger swallowed his beer and belched. "That kid claimed he was just here to talk to Robert Mueller. Said he was wandering around outside when the greybeard showed up. He hid under the deck when the guy started wandering around himself. Once the others showed up, he stayed in his hiding spot." He shrugged his wide shoulders, "One trespasser is the same as another." He turned back to the house and went inside.

Barney landed a couple of punches before the kid got his shit together and began to use the older man as a heavy bag. He wasn't using street fighting, the boy was doing some serious damage to Barney's body with kicks and flat fisted punches. Zippy had to turn his head away from Chaucer's sight, because Chaucer was still encouraging his boy to "beat that little motherfucker's ass." Baron had to stifle a smile when he watched Zippy pull his wallet from his back pocket and remove a few bills that he folded and slipped into his front pocket, before he put his wallet away.

The kid's punch to Barney's throat ended the battle. In less than six minutes, it was all over with. The boy walked over the man sitting in the grass clutching his throat, and staggered to the steps. He bent over with his hands on his knees to catch his breath. When he straightened, he scanned the faces of the men on the porch. He looked at Baron and said, "You are a hard man to find, and harder to talk to. My old man told me to come see you if I needed anything, and here I am. I sure hope you don't have another nutcase like that guy for me to fight before you'll consent to talk to me for a few minutes."

Almost everybody went about their business since the show was over. Baron waved Bobby Dee up the steps and offered him a seat. Zippy handed him a soda and slipped the money into the torn t-shirt pocket the boy was wearing. He nodded at him and walked off.

Baron looked at the kid. "Let's see if I have this right, your father is Darnell DeYoung. And since you're here and he isn't, my guess is that something went wrong in Afghanistan. My question is, what happened to your mother?"

Bobby looked at the man he was named after. This big guy made his six foot two father seem short. He grew up listening to stories about his father's best buddy, and seeing the man for himself, he was pretty sure his dad hadn't elaborated on their exploits much. "Dad bought it a year and a half ago. He was teamed with a dog named Zero, as in Zero tolerance. Both of them were targeted by the bastards. They were checking for bombs and explosives in a small village, and it was a trap. The letter from his commanding officer said he died a hero."

"Ten days ago, mom was in a car wreck. She caused the wreck that killed her. After dad died, she kept cursing the Army, and saying that dad loved it more than he loved us. She started drinking, and I think she decided to end it. I just graduated from high school in June, turned eighteen in July, and I guess I shouldn't have thought about joining the Army like my dad. Now she's gone, and in my dad's will, you were to get me if something happened to them. Technically, you don't get me, but you are the administrator of the will. There's money, but I don't know how much, and I can't touch it until I'm twenty-one. I want to go to the U of A, but again, I can't touch the money, and I can't get a grant or loan, because I can't demonstrate need. It's a clusterfucked up mess, so here I am."

*****

Baron finally climbed into bed at three in the morning. There were men lying on bedrolls in his living room, and in the spare bedrooms. Bobby Dee would stay with the Prospects in the basement at the club once the roads were passable. For now, he was sleeping in the corner of the living room with a couch pillow and a spare blanket.

Amy was sleeping on Gunner's shoulder, so he scooted under the covers to snuggle up against her backside. Hopefully she would feel better in the morning. The cheeks of her ass cradled his softened cock, and although it was beginning to act interested, he pushed the sensations back while drifting to sleep.

Gunner woke up when Amy rolled onto her back. He grabbed a pair of Baron's jeans that were an inch too long, but they would have to do until he got to his scooter. Hopefully the extra change of clothes hadn't gotten too wet from the damn rain. He took a leak in the master bathroom and looked at his reflection in the mirror when he scooped a handful of water over his face to help wake him up. His dark beard needed a trim, but that would have to wait. His brown eyes were a gift from his old man, but the girly dimples in his cheeks were from his mother. He wore the beard mainly to hide those dimples after being ragged on by the guys for being so pretty and cute. He rinsed his mouth with a swig of the blue stuff next to the sink and spit the burning shit out in the sink, and stood up. Seeing the left side of his chest that wasn't decorated with a tattoo yet, made him think about getting a new tat soon. Maybe not yet. He wasn't sure why he'd left the space empty, there just hadn't been anything worth documenting on his skin lately.

He almost stepped on Barney as he walked through the dining room. The man was lying on the floor, with his upper torso under the table and his legs were straight out, like he might have fallen over while asleep.

He found the coffee and brewed a pot. Someone had put the dishes away, and he figured it must have been Amy. Thoughts of her led him to remembering how good it felt to be inside of her pussy, and he had to redirect his thoughts, or go back to the bedroom and make a new memory to think about.

The rain was down to a drizzle now, but the forecast was calling for more thunderstorms. It was going to be a bitch riding the bike today, but they needed to get the prisoners away from Baron's personal property and take them to the club. He walked out to the carport and saw Zippy was babysitting the shivering wastes of space. If they were dried out and detoxed, there was a slim chance two of the five would live to see their next birthday. The kid under the silver blanket was Bruin's problem, if he came after his sister again he would be Gunner's, which meant he would die. For some reason, he'd allowed the evil tempered little witch to make him feel like she belonged to him and Baron, and neither man would allow someone to harm what was theirs.

Leech and Gator pulled onto the apron of the carport with the panel van. They came inside and helped themselves to the fresh coffee, and joined Gunner on the deck. It was cold out, but they wore jackets, Gunner was barefooted and bare chested, as if the cold didn't bother him at all.

Gator took a seat out of the worst of the wind and contemplated his boots while Leech and Gunner talked. They'd taken John Doe for his last ride, and Wally the Junkman had insisted they enjoy a beer or two before they left. The old man had a broken arm, and wasn't happy that his transportation was now his daughter. "She's a naggin' bitch, but she has stepped up and helped me a lot."

Tonight was the first time he'd used a backhoe and he still had traces of the white lime powder on his boot heels. They'd poured the shit over Reeker's body before covering him up. He wondered if the scraps of human waste huddling in the carport would be joining their leader soon. He wouldn't admit it, but he knew two of them. Oliver had been a nerd in school. He was one of those smart guys that everybody hated because he was the kind of

122

guy that reminded the teachers about homework assignments.

Pete was an ordinary guy in class. He was likeable, but never stood out in any one thing. Last Gator had heard about him, he'd taken on some heavy metal when an IED exploded in Iraq. Maybe he had brain damage. Who knew what men brought back from war with them.

He had not served, he washed out in the medical check. For some reason, he couldn't hear high-pitched noises. That was the least of his medical problems. The doctor told him that his heart was enlarged, and that was that for his career in the Army. He hadn't planned on any other future for himself. He wasn't particularly smart, and he wasn't born in a family with well-heeled parents. His mother worked two jobs just to keep a roof over their heads. The old man was absent since his mother came home from the hospital with his little sister. He'd dropped them off, and never came back.

Leech filled in the blanks for Gunner since he'd been busy taking care of Amy last night. He was envious of the men who got the privilege of watching Barney get his ass handed to him by a punk assed kid. The man would have been likeable if he didn't run his mouth so much. Maybe the ass whipping would slow him down, but it was doubtful.

"We need to take the trash down to the cooler and figure out what to do with them there. They can take some time to dry out there, and we won't have to babysit them so close then. Right now, I see five of them, so I hope we have the entire nest, I guess we'll find out sooner or later.

"Gator, you wanna find Preacher, then you can take the boys to the cellar? Hose 'em down when you get there, they've been pissing themselves and probably one or two of them shit their pants. I can't stand the smell of puke, and when they start suffering, they will be puking and shitting. You ever see a junkie try to claw his scalp off? They'll be begging for someone to shoot them by tomorrow. The trick is to not shoot them, no matter how tempted you might be."

# CHAPTER TWELVE

She was enjoying the feel of a man's mouth on her breast, sucking and teasing the nipple with teeth and an agile tongue. It felt like heaven to have a man's hands shaping the large mounds of flesh, while the pull of his sucking tingled straight to her womb. This was a wonderful way to be awakened from her dream of the two sexy men.

She knew she was wet, ready for his prick, but he kept teasing her breasts. "Hey, I love what you're doing there, but I need you to take a detour down south if you happen to feel up to it." Her fingers were playing with his hair, and her other hand's fingers were slowly rubbing her clit.

His big hand abandoned one of her breasts, and traveled down to meet with her damp fingers. He pressed her fingers harder over the small muscle, and extended his own to hook inside of her tight vaginal entrance. He pulled with those fingers, and added another finger to the soaked flesh. She felt like pumping her hips, the need to get the friction moving for the orgasm that was waiting for her to do her part. Pleasure was waiting and she wanted it. "Yes, like that, just a little faster, oh please don't stop." Her words of encouragement made Baron grin. He wasn't about to let her get too happy. He planned to fuck her into the mattress, and wanted to feel her tight cunt grab his prick while he spilled his load deep inside of her.

He pulled his fingers from her hole and lifted his mouth from her tit. Her narrow eyed expression made him laugh. "Calm down, Stretch, I'm gonna fuck you. I think you need to learn to be patient." He took her hand from her clit and pulled the other hand from her breast. "Let me take a minute to look at you, all this smooth skin and curves makes me want to shove my cock deep and stay there for a while." He pushed one long leg between hers and said, "Spread them, if I have to do it for you, I might add a few swats to this pretty little pussy for your disobedience. I thought we'd established that I like to be in charge." Her thighs opened wide and he nodded at her. "Good girl, now raise those legs up and grab them with your hands behind your knees, don't fuck around, my prick's about to shoot cum all over you, and if that happens, you're gonna have a reason to say I'm a selfish fucker."

She had no choice but to watch as he split her open with his thumbs and looked up to see her watching. He said, "Watch this," it was his thick cock head sliding between his thumbs as it pushed its way inside of her vaginal tunnel. "Fuck this is tight, your pussy is almost chewing at my cock."

He was right, seconds after he began sliding into her depths, her channel clamped down and released rhythmically as she came. Her head was thrown back, and her jaw was clenched while she rode out her orgasm with very little noise. The smack on her clit made her gasp and open her eyes.

"You don't fucking keep that shit behind your teeth, I can feel it, I wanna hear it. Now do it again, but do it right this time." He slammed the last few inches inside of her and she whimpered.

The orgasm had primed her and made her delicate inner flesh sensitive. His cock was stretching over those twitching bundles of nerves and her hips jerked. She cried out when he hit bottom, but shoved her hips up to encourage him even more. "That's right, let me hear it. Let all the motherfuckers in this place hear my name coming out of your mouth." She couldn't hold back any longer. He kept saying possessive domineering shit, but she liked it, more than she'd ever thought she might. Telling her to "Take every fucking inch of it," and then he bit her on the shoulder, kept her mind on her body. His cock kissed her cervix, and it was enough to shove her over the edge. She felt his prick pushing the milky liquid from his body into the mouth of her womb, as she screamed his name, just like he'd said she would.

*****

She was becoming waterlogged from all of the baths and showers she'd had in the last two days. Her feet had gotten the worst of the injuries, and every time she stepped down, the thin cuts would split longer and some would bleed. As soon as she was cleaned up, Baron dressed her in another pair of his boxers that he never used, and a black t-shirt declaring freedom is two wheels and an open road. She was still self-conscious about being carried around, after all she was no lightweight. Her attempts to move around on her own got her nowhere but it did get her a quick five smacks on her ass. She conceded with a comment. "All right, if you have to play the caveman, go for it, but don't whine to me about your aching back later."

She met Bruin and although he still frightened her, he assured her that David was going to be rehabbed. "I'll be taking him with me, and he's going to learn to live without that shit poisoning what few brain cells he has left." He didn't think she needed to know that David was in for a couple of weeks of hell. "You are prettier than your mother ever was, taller too. I always thought you were a cute kid."

What could she say besides thank you. She was relieved that her brother would be taken in hand and with someone who seemed to care about his welfare. "Thank you for taking care of him."

Gunner refused to allow her to tell her brother goodbye. "Wait until he is cleaned up. The next time you see him, he will be a whole new person. I have a feeling that his old man will work him into a man you could probably be proud of. Right now, all you will remember is a bag of bones with a fat lip. Give him time, leaving him a scrap of dignity won't hurt you, and it might help him."

Bruin agreed whole-heartedly. "A man has demons, you need to let him wrestle with his for a while. I'll let you know when he's ready to see you again. He owes you, but he has to learn about himself before he takes on a woman's issues." He nodded at her and the rest of the people in the room and left the house. He was wearing a rain poncho, and carried a plastic trash bag in his hand for David's use to keep the rain off some. The cold wet ride would do the boy good. He'd be one miserable asshole by the time they stopped tonight.

They heard the bike rumble and she went to the door to watch them leave. She felt like crying, but held back her tears. She should have done more to keep David clean herself. She hated the knowledge that he was with a virtual stranger, it didn't matter that Bruin was his father. He'd never been around while David was growing up, even though he knew of his son's existence. Hopefully, this act of parenthood wasn't too much too late. She turned to look at the men sitting around the big room with the few items of furniture. It was time for her to go home and pick up her life. She could hang around the apartment until the insurance company decided to determine what they would do. With David gone, and no other witnesses, they should pay for the building to be rebuilt. Sadly, the Swinger was only insured for property damage. She couldn't afford to insure it for what it was really worth, so she would need to find a new vehicle.

She had thought about it and decided to have the building rebuilt along the same set up that it was before the fire. She could live above the business, and that would save a lot of money each month, so she could actually afford car payments. That should work out pretty good. She went looking for Baron and found him talking to his club brothers, they seemed to be having a meeting, and she knew she wasn't welcome. Gunner jerked his head sideways for her to leave. She didn't argue. If she had a way to leave the property completely, she would be out of here.

She rummaged through the cupboards and found pancake mix and decided to fix herself something to eat. Since she knew Baron hadn't had time to scavenge anything for breakfast, she decided to make extra for him, knowing that most men would eat anything they didn't have to cook, she decided to be nice and cook the entire box of mix, what didn't get eaten could always go in the fridge for tomorrow if Baron wanted them. She mixed the buttermilk pancake mix and pulled a barstool over to the stove. She had this, no problem.

There was a mountain of pancakes sitting on the counter by the time the men came looking for her. She had to snatch two of the cakes for herself before the mass of muscle grabbed them all. Baron slapped a big bottle of syrup down and helped himself to the paper plates, and a pile of pancakes. She was surprised that some of the men ate like starving wolves. No one was planning to take the food off their plates for crissakes. Preacher insisted on saying a prayer over the food. It was a good thing that his head was bowed and his eyes were closed in his sincere prayer, since several men filled their faces before his Amen was said.

She moved her stool to the counter breakfast bar and ate her flat cakes and drank a hot cup of coffee. She was happy there were plenty of paper plates and plastic forks to go around, even if some of the men picked up the pancakes and ate them like a slice of bread. Not that she planned to clean the place again. One go around was enough for her. It was a beautiful home though. She could imagine sitting by the fireplace enjoying a drink with Baron, and Gunner. *That kind of thinking will only lead to trouble, girlie.* To daydream about a fantasy relationship with the two of them was pretty harmless, doing it too often would lead to heartache.

The rain let up, and the weather report said there was more to come in the late afternoon. Everyone decided to take a chance and go to the clubhouse, or their own homes. She blushed when almost every man thanked her for cooking. That puzzled her, with so many of the club's women there, how come none of them wanted to cook, aside from Bernie's goulash that was. "Oh well, it's not your problem now is it?" she asked herself. If they were this grateful for something as simple as pancakes, how grateful would they be for a real home cooked meal?

Amy gathered the shirt and shorts that belonged to Charm, and the fuck me boots belonging to Freddie, and put them in a plastic bag. She'd washed the clothes when she washed Baron's clothes. She was adequately covered for now, at least until she could get into her apartment and change into her own clothing.

She watched the bikes leave and had to admit to herself that she envied the men riding the big machines. She'd only been on a bike twice in her life now, but she loved it. Baron's arms came around her from behind and she smiled. "I have had a very interesting time with you these past couple of days. I almost hate to go back to real life." She laughed a little. "Let's hope the apartment manager hasn't evicted me after all the problems this week. There is a clause in the lease about being disruptive to the other tenants. I might have to get a police report to show them, and hope they find some good in their hearts and let me stay."

His lips skimmed the skin under her ear and drifted down her neck. She leaned into the caress. She wanted to say screw it and fall back into that huge bed in the other room with him and stay there for the entire day. The problem with that would be the same reluctance to go home the next day. She pulled back from his arms, and he let her go.

He looked unhappy when she turned to say something else, and she decided not to poke his grump buttons. What his problem was she had no idea, and she didn't want to get involved any more than she was in his life. She watched Gunner walk into the room and she tried a smile for him, he smiled back, but it was a reserved smile, and she knew it was time to go. If she stayed, she was in for heartbreak.

She walked to the door and waited for them to make up their minds whether to chance the bikes or drive the dually. Baron looked at her feet and pulled out the truck keys. Gunner carried her out to the truck, depositing her into the back seat, before going to his bike and opening the saddlebags to get her purse.

The ride to her apartment was almost silent. She asked them if there was time in the schedule to drive past her building downtown, and Baron parked in front of the burned out shell of the place she'd built her business in. There was yellow police tape surrounding the building, and orange plastic netting to keep curious busybodies out of the mess.

"This makes me sick to look at, I worked my ass off for my business. It wasn't a lot, but it was mine. I hope the insurance comes through." She was too choked to talk any longer. The blackened shell showed her that nothing was forever. Even a building constructed of brick. Being alone sucked.

They drove to her apartment, and sure enough, there was an eviction taped to her graffiti adorned door. It wasn't fair, but she understood. Where she would find another apartment until the building was rebuilt was anyone's guess. The notice gave her a generous seven days to leave. Gunner came in behind her while Baron looked around outside before he entered the apartment.

"It's no wonder he didn't have any problem breaking in here. The screens are flexible, and the windows can be popped out with a little effort. You're better off moving out of here anyway."

She couldn't figure out what put him in such a good mood since they'd left his house. He was almost smiling while telling her that she was better off finding a new home? This was the only apartment complex in the town. Not to mention that she needed to get the insurance company to expedite her claim, and she had no vehicle to move her things if she did have a place to go. It was her time to be gloomy and damn it, he was taking that away because she was enjoying his smile too much to worry about her immediate future. Gunner was wandering through the apartment, but she could see an identical look on his lips as Baron's.

"Go ahead and make your phone calls, we'll be back in a little while with lunch, how does that sound?" The sneaky ass was up to something, Gunner hadn't shown his dimples that she could remember. The beard hid them some, but she could see them and knew he was up to no good. Baron was already through the door, before she got a good look at him. She didn't have time to dwell on the dimples, or the wide chests and long legs of her, what? She couldn't label them her lovers. They'd shared a very enjoyable sexual encounter. And this morning with Baron, had been the ice cream on the apple pie, but she couldn't very well call them her boyfriends. There was nothing boyish about them.

It was a puzzle for another time, right now she needed to get her priorities in order. She looked up her insurance papers and picked up the phone. A half an hour later, she was so mad she was threatening the Better Business Bureau, or a lawyer, since a family member was the number one suspect in the arson, they wouldn't pay her a dime until he was proven innocent, and someone else was arrested. They would do a site cleanup, but they refused to give her a penny until their investigation was complete and David was in the clear. Her car wasn't covered for vandalism, as she already knew.

When Gunner walked in with a pizza and a six pack, she grabbed the beer first. Baron came in with an armload of boxes for her to pack her things. She told them of her conversation with the insurance company, and almost choked on her pizza when Baron asked her if she wanted him to kill the smartass agent who had been so nasty to her. "I can take him out without him even seeing me. You just say the word and he's toast."

# CHAPTER THIRTEEN

She was finally alone. The men were reluctant to leave her by herself, until she pointed out that she had been living and enjoying her life in the apartment far longer than she'd known them. "I have a life, it's just gone in a different direction for now. I will be fine. My credit is pretty good, I have a client list, and if I have to, I will rent a building for my business until they decide to pay up. It's not like I can go to them and tell them that David did burn my building down, but he is going to stop being a naughty boy now that his daddy has taken him in hand."

She now had both men's cell phone numbers programmed in her phone, and had to promise them that she would call if she needed anything. They'd enjoyed a "quickie" before the men left. Her pussy was still soaked from coming twice, while she sucked Baron's cock, and Gunner's prick pounded deep inside of her vagina. Even an hour after they left, she could feel the delicious tingles lingering through her body.

She cleaned up, got one of the beers the men had left, and opened the laptop. She had to find a place to live, and get estimates for reopening her business. It would take days to get herself together, but she was a person who thrived on a deadline.
*****

Baron sat in the office at the club with Gunner, Burger, and Leech. They were having a talk on the phone with their ex-President, War. After informing the man that had truly become more of a brother to each man, of the happenings around the area, Baron brought up a subject that needed to be dealt with.

"Do you remember that brother we brought back with us from Wolfman's camp by the name of Lloyd? He's been asking questions, questions that he has no business asking. He asked one of the trial members about a bag of bling. Now as far as I knew, only you and I knew where that particular bag went to. Right?"

War was not surprised to hear that bit of news. "I figured as much, but hoped he wasn't the snitch. Wolfman knows that certain factions in the club are looking to maybe replace him. I'm not the only Prez he has here. That fat fucker Gordon from Kansas, and there is a guy from the north in Michigan that they call King Ben. Both of them are mean motherfuckers. I saw Ferdinand two days ago, and Rambo is here too. Something is up, and I watch my back as well as keeping track of the rest of them. It fuckin' sucks that I have no backup here.

"I'd lay out good money that Wolfy has sent men to each of their clubs to ferret out information. The son-of-a-bitch is trying to cause shit in the clubs so he can step in and save the day. He needs to look like he's worth keeping in the chair, but there is a lot of opposition."

Gunner spoke up, "How about a couple of the boys show up bringing you a gift. You know, something to entertain the bastards for a few days. Say five dopers that might or might not be worth drying out and recruiting? If we dispose of them here, it might cause a dust up, but if we let it be known they are traveling east, no one will question it too much if they disappear from the radar. Our boys will be there to help you for a week or two, and maybe things can become a little clearer with three sets of eyes instead of one."

They finalized the plans and Gunner was turned down for trying to volunteer. "I appreciate the offer, man, but send me Barney and Chaucer. They are expendable if shit hits the fan here. They will fit right in with the lunatics that surround Wolf now."

Burger and Leech left the room to expedite the plans. Barney was probably drunk by now, and trying to pretend that a kid almost half his age hadn't handed him his ass last night.

"Oh yeah, thought you might want to know, Caroline made the rounds here, the whore tried to get me to fuck her too. When I told her it wasn't happening, she had her own little version of a gangbang with Wolf and his closest six friends. She ended up in the hospital. Two days later, she was back and higher than fuck. She took a few too many of her Oxy's and died sometime during another fuck fest. The sick bastard that was screwing her at the time, finished his shit before he left her corpse." He waited to hear what they had to say, but silence was all that met his ears. "I'm sorry, I know you three were close for a while."

Baron spoke, his voice was even, even if he was shaking his head at the waste of her life. "Maybe she can find peace in death. She dropped me and Gunner because we refused to take our fists to her face and body. I would have had no problem if she wanted fist fucked, but I don't fuck up women for

137

no reason, you feel me? If a bitch deserves it I'll deal with punishing her, or choose another option."

Gunner spoke up too. "Fuck, War, you know what kinky sons-a-bitches we are. She could take whatever we dished out and begged for more. I'm glad she was there when she bought it and not here. If that sounds cold, it's because she burned her bridges a long time ago with me."

They disconnected not long after that and sat looking at each other. Caroline's needs had made them question their own. Now she was dead, and they each knew that she had been dead to them for a long time. Way before she finally left, that was for sure.

Those thoughts brought the subject of Amy into the front of their minds, and Baron finally voiced his plans for her. "I plan to have Stretch as a permanent fixture around here as soon as I can find a way to get her to like the idea. Something about her gets me hard every time I see her, and I get a kick out of seeing her in the kitchen. If you're in, say so. If not, I can understand that you need to find one of your own that you don't have to share. We've been a team for a long time, and I hate to lose you, but when she was lying in that big bed, it felt right, you know? I walked in the room dead tired, and she was lying with her head on your shoulder, I snugged up behind her, and it just felt like home. Sounds girly when I say that out loud, but it is what it is."

Gunner grinned halfway through his best friend's speech. "Man, I was going to say almost the exact same thing to you about her. I don't own a house, but shit, I have the money to buy one if I need to. I can pay half of the bills, and we can continue living the lifestyle we enjoy. Now that we cleared the air, we need a plan." Melvin perked his head up from his position on the couch. He hopped down and jumped onto Gunner's lap. It was the first time the little fur ball had come near Gunner since he'd bitten the man. "Oh sure, you come around when your favorite slave's name is mentioned right? Fine, just remember, you bite me again, you're going to be a clubhouse pet, and be forced to eat scraps and live with those damn cats you rescued." Melvin didn't look worried.

First things first, Club business, then personal concerns. They took the truck back to Baron's place and mounted up on the bikes. Baron was carrying a little extra something, just in case. Anytime he transported income, he was cautious. They drove for a few miles and turned off onto a dirt two track. Gunner signaled to Baron to pull over for a confab. They shut the scooters down and Baron looked annoyed at the interruption. "What?"

"I don't know, man, something's off. My fuckin' guts are burning like a son-of-a-bitch. I got the feeling a couple of miles back, it's a damned creepy feeling crawling along my neck. I'm not saying let's turn back or anything, but I think we should wait for a few."

Baron stared at him for a few seconds, he'd known Gunner for most of his adult life, and one thing was certain. Gunner had instincts that no one in their right mind would ignore. If he said something was wrong, it was gospel. There was very little brush or any thick groupings of trees to secret the bikes behind, so they lined them together and scuffed the ground nearby leading into the woods. They found a spot on the opposite side of the two track in a big pine. They could see anything around them from twenty feet up. Both men were armed, and ready to see what was coming.

They waited a good ten minutes before they heard the sounds of bikes coming their way. Two flat black rat bikes and one decent looking crotch rocket came down the small lane toward the big bikes. The rider of the royal blue rocket dismounted from his perch and the two others joined him. They looked around and found the spot where it appeared the big men had gone into the woods. They all pulled guns from their waistbands and pockets. When they started to sneak into the woods, crouching and trying to stay low, Gunner sighed. He and Baron knew what they needed to do. It was a shame that their afternoon would be taken up having to deal with turncoats and druggies.

*****

Burger drove the panel van, leading a troupe of five bikes. Lloyd and his new found friends ran out of the woods to their bikes when they heard the motors disturbing the peaceful countryside. They met the brothers next to the bikes, and had put their weapons away before exiting the cover of the long weeds and trees. Leech and Burger listened as the three men told them that they were concerned about Baron and Gunner. They were too nervous to notice that four men walked up behind them and grabbed them in bear hugs until Burger hit each man with a taser. Gunner watched the finesse the easygoing Burger used to render his victims into screaming twitching bitch boys. He laid the small black box on each man's neck in turn, and when he said release him, the brother would drop his arms and stand back, while Burger gleefully hit the on button. They were tied up and tossed into the back of the van, before the bikes and van backed out of the road and headed back to the clubhouse.

Baron split his pants coming down out of the tree. They were covered in sticky pine tar, and had several scratches to show for their adventure. They continued on their way after a lot of cussing and complaining. The place called Honeycomb Hill was a dangerous place for the unwary. Years ago, when precious stones were found in the north end of the state, there were individual miners who sought to strike it rich in the mining of those stones. They would dig down as far as the bedrock, and created a honeycomb of twenty-foot deep mines. Some were quite large under the surface of the ground above them, and several people had lost their lives by falling into a hole that was covered by the long grasses growing on the hilltop.

Once they stopped, Baron changed his jeans, it pissed him off about the jeans, they were only a few months old. Cheap shit.

They were headed to one particular mine. The man who greeted them was a total whack job. He had a thing for metal, the more expensive the metal the better he liked it. They upended the bag of jewelry in a tub, and Midas started pawing through the chains and watches. If it wasn't for the fact that

Baron needed to pick up the melted and formed bars of platinum, gold, and silver, he wouldn't have spoken to them further. He was lost in the land of shiny objects, and that was why he'd been living in this hole in the ground for five years. The Breed always brought him new shinnies, and their dedication to his craft, was gratifying. Midas was a find, War had found him somewhere out west, and allowed him to sift his fingers through the ten pound box of non-marketable jewelry. Midas named his price, and now belonged to the Breed. He didn't leave the place unless he needed to go to town to buy food or whatever else he might need to live. He was like a mother hen with the objects they bought to him. The Club was happy, and for the price of a clean pierced pussy once a month plus a cut of the sale, he was cheap labor.

Baron special ordered a gift and explained what he wanted, while Midas nodded his head and grinned. His saddlebag was put into use to carry the small gold ingots, and Gunner had a smaller bag of diamonds and other gems, another containing the guts from the watches. Both bags would be dropped off with the gold to the Jewelry Exchange. It was a legit business, with an easy way of laundering money in solid metal form.

They left the odd little man, and headed to town. Gunner had his mind on the three men who followed them earlier. He didn't see the buck come running out of the ditch on the side of the road. The animal collided with the side of the motorcycle and Gunner went down. He landed on his side with the bike on his leg, and pain so bad from his shoulder, that it took everything he had to stop himself from screaming.

Baron doubled back when he heard the crash of metal on concrete. Fuck, Gunner was down, and a ten point buck was on his front knees, flopping back and forth, trying to get up. He parked his bike and ran to where Gunner was laying. Thankfully he was alive and awake. He turned the key off to shut down the motor. He yanked the handlebars and seat, removing the heavy scooter off his best friend, and could see that Gunner needed an ambulance. The bone in his leg was showing through a grisly bloody mess of meat and muscle.

He tried to roll onto his back, but that wasn't happening, the pain was excruciating. "Fucking shoot that bastard. Call the brothers and have them gut it. No sense in leaving good meat to rot on the side of the fuckin' road. Fuck, my damn shoulder is broke or worse. My goddamned hip feels like I've been shot. Sorry to let you down, buddy, but I'm gonna be laid up for a while. Fuck, this is fucked up. My skull is pounding like a son-of-a-bitch."

Baron let him ramble; as long as he was talking, he was alive, and he could run his pie hole for an hour if that's what it took to keep him alive until the ambulance could get there. He'd called 911 once he had seen the leg, then he called the Clubhouse. He took Gunner's semi auto .45 and put a bullet in the beautiful buck's brain.

Myrtle cussed him for discharging the gun while her ear was so close to the noise coming from the phone. "Sorry, Gunner's down, and we need a truck to haul his trophy. The fucker went hunting with his bike. Bagged a ten pointer. His bike is intact, but might need some attention too, so tell them to call John to meet us here. I'll follow the medics to the hospital and keep you up to date." He started to quit the connection, and remembered Melvin, "Hey, you mind taking care of Mel for me tonight?" She called him a dick and hung up on him.

He went back to Gunner, "You know there's easier ways to get a few weeks off. Like maybe telling me you're leaving for vacation? By the way, that is one majestic son-of-a-bitch you got there. Gonna have that rack mounted and put on the wall at the club." He heard the meat wagon's siren screaming through the early evening quiet. Gunner was out of his head, and couldn't form a coherent sentence by now, so he didn't bother asking him if he was carrying another piece. Gunner was always prepared. It felt strange searching his buddy, but found a belly gun and a toad sticker in his boot, and the one on his belt. The coiled garrote was added to his collection of weapons. He took them and the saddlebags to his bike. It might have been difficult to explain most of the items to curious civilians. He took the wad of cash, and sliced his own knife through the belt loop holding the chain attached to Gunner's wallet. No way would he allow some stranger to pilfer through his best friend's personal shit.

The ambulance finally stopped twenty feet from the bike and Baron was yelling at the EMTs. "Get your asses over here, he needs to go now. Load his big ass up and get him to the hospital." They brought a backboard with them, and under normal circumstances, he might find the idea of the two volunteer medics attempting to pick up and carry his two hundred fifty pound friend hilarious, right now, it pissed him off. He grabbed the board and shoved it as far under Gunner's body as he could, before rolling his shaking body on top of the rigid surface.

The older medic told him repeatedly to back off. He finally nodded his head and stood back while they worked on their patient. He was pressed into service lifting the oversized man onto the gurney and shoving it into the back of the truck. He gave the driver Gunner's license and insurance card before they left with sirens screaming.

Two scoots and a pick-up pulled around him within minutes of the ambulance leaving. The police car showed up about the same time and took pictures of the bike and dead deer. It was a damned waste of time as far as Baron could see. He wanted to be on his bike and headed to the hospital, but he still had to deliver the merchandise, and get himself under control.

# CHAPTER FOURTEEN

Two days after the accident, Baron was standing at Amy's door. He needed her help, and she needed a place to park. If they could make her fall in with their plans, she would become a cherished house mouse. Gunner was in for a long convalescence, to the tune of a couple of months at the very least. The doctors had to pin his leg together, his hip had been dislocated, and he would need another surgery to get his shoulder back in working order. If she came with him to get the house ready for Gunner to stay, there was no going back. He had six Prospects and two trucks waiting his call to move her sweet ass out to the house.

She answered the door and felt a sense of panic when she saw his face. "What happened?" She grabbed his hand and he let her haul him inside the doorframe. She looked around outside of the door, but didn't see Gunner anywhere.

"Where is he? Tell me, what happened, it's Gunner, isn't it?" She knew her voice was getting higher, but fuck it. She was already having a shitty day. She couldn't find a place to move into, and the only buildings suitable for her to re-open her business were way out of her price range. The insurance company was still holding out, and the lawyer she'd talked to told her they were legally in their rights, she would have to wait them out, or move on. She'd just finished crying and washing her face when Baron knocked on her door.

He pulled her into his strong arms. "He's alive, and he will be pretty messed up for a while, but he's going to be alright. He's looking at a long recovery." He told her about the deer and the lousy past few days. "I came here to see you, and to ask you for a favor."

The trucks were loaded with her meager furniture and boxes of personal stuff that were already packed. Baron told Leech to make sure everything was treated gently and stored in one of the spare bedrooms, and her couch and tables were to go into his living room. She nodded at him and wiped her nose. She was on the verge of tears again, and pissed at herself for showing so much emotion.

Amy insisted on stopping at the hospital to see Gunner before they drove out to the house. When she saw him lying against the white cotton, she lost it. She walked to the end of his bed, and only Baron could see her clenched fists, while she lectured the sleeping man in broken words between gulps of air. "Damn you, you have to ride that damn bike all over the countryside during deer season. You both are lucky you weren't shot by a stray bullet. What were you thinking, it was dusk, you guys were on motorized bicycles, and you know the deer are being run by dogs and men. I hope your pride is worth the pain. If you'd been in a truck, at least you might not have gotten so busted up." She came around the bed and stood by his side, reaching out to touch his bruised face. Her thumb lightly rubbed over the beard covered dimple. "If you die, I'm gonna bitch slap your ass all the way to hell." She leaned down and kissed his lips before turning to leave the room.

For the first time in days, Baron grinned. Gunner opened one eye, looking sideways. "Did she say yes?" He closed his eye when Baron told him yes. "That's a plus, what the hell, bitch slap me?" He coughed and smiled as he fell back to sleep.

*****

They stopped off for dinner at the steak house. She devoured the first decent meal she'd eaten in weeks. Baron was happy to see that his woman liked her food and didn't pick at a lone lettuce leaf and announce that it was too filling, or some such shit. She drank a beer with her meal just as if they'd been syncing each other's likes for years.

They talked about the arrangements for Gunner's homecoming and his care. "Well, I've never been around someone who needs constant nursing, but I promise to try my best. I can't imagine that he is a good patient now, I might need a taser or bullwhip in a few weeks."

On the way home, Baron thought about Amy and the very real possibility that she would be a permanent fixture in their lives. He needed to talk to her about what would be expected from her when they were at the clubhouse, or in a group of people. She was going to balk at the respect thing, but she needed to know and be on board with the program, or his and Gunner's plans for her in their future would never work.

As their old lady, she would go from being a novelty to being a club princess, and that brought responsibility. The real Queen of the group of old lady's was Vern's old lady, Furfur. She was the eldest and had been with the club the longest. She was a mean old bitty, but there wasn't a member of the brotherhood that would not die for her.

When they drove into the carport, she felt as if she was now home. Technically she was, at least for the foreseeable future. She needed to talk with Baron and set some limits. There was no question in her mind they would be having sex on a regular basis. Just as she knew that, her soul would be shattered when it was time for her to leave. It was a sorry state of her make-up, but she half suspected that she was falling in love with the men. Even sorrier was the fact she knew it and was stepping forward, and might as well be wearing a sign that said whore in big bold letters on her forehead. She was addicted to the big cocks that just happened to be attached to a couple of even bigger pricks that had the ability to make her heart smile.

It surprised her when Baron told her to make herself at home and start a list of groceries that she might need or want to cook for meals. "Look around, if you need something, put it on the list. He showed her where the deep freezer was, and she was impressed with the amount of game meat that she saw. Pheasants, turkey, and venison, not to mention several plastic bags of filet fish, made her want to start unpacking her pots and pans. She loved to cook and now she would have a reason.

"I need to be at the club in a few, I'll be back tonight. He started to walk out of the door and turned around, grabbed her shoulders and pulled her close enough for a quick mouth fuck. "Be in my bed naked when I get home. I like the feel of your skin."

She stood where he left her as he walked out of the door. She noticed that he locked the door behind him, and got a sappy smile on her tingling lips. It was still early, so she found the room that contained her boxes, and carried the kitchen things to the counter. It took her an hour to clean everything and put her dishes into the cupboard, she took particular pleasure in unpacking and putting away her cooking pans.

She took a long hot bath and relaxed for the first time in days. The idea of living here, taking care of the house and men, appealed to her feminine side. The knowledge that she would get as much of her brand of sex as she wished made her decision to stay for a while seem even more like the right choice. She climbed onto the big bed, and used the remote to flip through the channels. Seeing three porn stations didn't surprise her, but she watched a particularly raunchy scene for a few minutes before changing the channel to a late night talk show. Somehow, the funny man sent her to sleep.

*****

The building choice was a good one. It was isolated enough that no one would notice the fire burning until the place was engulfed in flames. It was also far enough outside of town that there were no fire hydrants and water would need to be trucked in.

Baron stood back watching the flames lick the old paint on the outside of the building. Lloyd had been a hard ass to the end. Taking his knife to the

150

man's cock and balls loosened his tongue a little, but not enough. The two assholes with him only knew that he'd promised them a wad of cash for helping him recover money that he claimed had been stolen from him. They were shit eaters, and cried like babies when they saw his blades. Baron liked to make sure those who he killed remained dead. The knives lying on each man's Adam's Apple and pulled in opposite directions, sliced cleanly and deep.

Lloyd watched the coffin bait die with no expression. He smiled at Baron and Leech as they came for him. He thought he would get away with his throat slit, but the big men knew that. They used their imagination to get information from their victims. Right now, he was wishing they weren't so crazy. Especially that big motherfucker, Baron. That fucker grinned while he'd sliced those boys up.

"I ain't telling you shit, go ahead, and slice my throat. A man's gotta die sometime, tonight looks like a good night to go as far as I can tell." When his pants and shirt were sliced off his body by the pretty boy they called Leech, he figured he was in for an old fashioned ass reaming. He didn't bother to tell them that that ship had sailed years ago. He was bi-sexual, so at least his last minutes on earth might be pleasurable. He didn't expect the dual knives wielded by that crazy fucker to slice through the flesh surrounding his cock.

Baron was careful to cut at the precise angles for maximum pain. He knew the son-of-a-bitch expected an easy death. "Surprised? Now why would you be surprised that you are being taken out for attempting to steal from and probably kill me?" He stood back and let Leech at their victim.

"Now you see here, I tried to welcome you to the group, and even got Bernie to give you one of her specialty blowjobs. I'm gonna have to send her a box of candy to get the taste of a traitor out of her mouth. I happen to like ol' Baron here, he and I bonded over bitches and beer many times. Ain't that right, buddy?" Baron nodded his head and handed Leech a beer, then clicked bottles and saluted each other before upending the beer and swallowing it down without stopping. He tossed the bottle into the corner and went back to the ugly fucker that was standing in a small pool of his own blood. "I say you are working for ol' Wolfman; Baron here, well he thinks you're just a thieving asshole, but he thinks someone would sweeten your wallet if you killed him and you could keep the gold for yourself." He stepped closer, "Truth is, you ain't gonna leave this building, it's up to you how you leave this world. You like pain? You came to the right place. You wanna tell us how and why you found out about the gold, and why you tried to ambush our President, I promise you a quick death. No more slices into your skin like this one." He stuck his knife in Lloyd's chest, and sliced through his nipple and down to his last rib.

Leech was picking up a gallon of bleach that was at his side on top of a pile of old tires, and poured half of it over Lloyd's head. The burning cleaner dribbled in his eyes, and he screamed, but his executioners stood back and smiled as they watched the liquid trail down his chest, making its way to the bloody slices in his skin. Their victim didn't stop screaming until Baron slapped him hard. "What the fuck, man, women use the shit all of the time, I never seen one scream and whine like that. Better suck it up fucker, there's still half a gallon left." He shrugged his shoulders and nodded at Leech, who poured the rest of the corrosive over him again.

Their victim screamed, but wasn't talking, so Baron showed Lloyd the wallet that had been in his pocket when he was taken. "Leech, look at this, the back of this picture of a pretty girl says, 'To Uncle Lloyd, the best uncle a girl could have'. It's signed Rebecca Ann Dryer. Can you read the sign in the background of the picture? Does that say Ingrid Heights? I wonder if she'd like a ride on a real bike, she'll look good dancing on a pole at the club, right?"

That got a reaction from Lloyd, he started fighting, the harder he fought his bonds, the more his wounds bled. Baron reached out and slapped him up side his head. "Tell me what I want to know, or I will send Chaucer and Barney to pick her up, I'm not fuckin' with you about this. Tell me what I want to know, or what happens to her is on you. It's as simple as that. You'll be dead, and she will be property for any cock that wants her. I might even be moved to send her to Wolfman and his posse, you know how much they like the tender young cunts like your niece, right? Isn't Wolf the one that grabs girls off the streets and keeps them chained in his meth labs after they're too worn out to be fucked anymore? By the time she's twenty-five, Wolf will have fucked her and every one of his personal guard will have too. Hell, I remember old Wolfy fuckin' a young girl up bad, so bad, that she had to shit in a bag for almost a year before she was healed enough to do it the old fashioned way. I wonder how Rebecca will enjoy his fist up her ass?"

Lloyd had very few scruples, he didn't believe in God, he'd stopped believing in his Country, and the only thing that meant anything was that girl. "Alright, Wolfman wants you dead. He wants to start what he calls civil unrest." He coughed and spit on the floor. "Don't feel special, asshole, five others are doing the same thing I am in the southern clubs. All you motherfuckers are gonna fuckin' die. That's all I know, so kill me, or let me go."

There was no way he would have carried out his threats, and he actually had no idea what Wolf did to his whores, rumors were plenty, but no one had actually told him anything, so whatever he told Lloyd, was a complete lie. No way would he harm an innocent, but the man in front of him didn't know that.

Baron nodded his head. Leech was busy unscrewing the caps from camping fuel and sloshing some around, just a little, so the fire would have a chance to lick up the papers and barrels filled with used motor oil. Nine rat bikes and Lloyd's scooter were lined up nearby. Lloyd began screaming names at the two men, but they went about their business. When it was time for them to leave, Leech came near the man that hoped for death. "Did you know they say the last thing that dies in a man is his brain? You are one lucky sumbitch, when you get to hell, you can tell the devil that you got a taste of his place already so throw your ass in the pit."

He didn't see which man tossed the roman candle into the middle of the room. He was too busy attempting to get loose from the ropes. His blood was still dripping down onto his prick and balls, and his last coherent thoughts were of his countless misdeeds over the years. Retribution and that bitch Karma had caught up to him. His screams of pain could be heard from outside where the two men stood watching the flames. Small explosions could be heard as the bikes, or cans of fuel, caught the attention of the hungry flames.

They waited close by to make sure the fire had done its job, before Leech made an anonymous call to the authorities before they mounted up and rode away.

The men drove to Baron's place. It was already four in the morning, and both men needed to clean up before anyone saw them. They'd gone into the kitchen and started shucking their shirts, washing the taste of smoke from their throats with a beer.

Baron locked up and told Leech to shower in the weight room downstairs and take the first room in the hallway to sleep in. He went into the guest shower between the two empty rooms and soaped his body and hair twice before he was satisfied the smell and blood from his night's work was washed down the drain. The clothes he and Leech had shed went into the washer along with the towels, he turned the dial on after he added a generous amount of soap to the load.

# CHAPTER FIFTEEN

Amy woke to the feeling of a man's beard tickling her thighs. She sat up and was immediately pushed back down. "Relax, Stretch, I need the taste of you and when I've had enough of your pussy in my mouth, I plan to fuck you until neither of us can fuckin' twitch." His fingers pulled the lips of her pussy back and he held them, pinching them while his teeth scraped and his tongue fucked her hole. He let go of the lips and it felt as if he was trying to eat through her flesh to get to the tender center. He bit, and shoved two fingers deep. "I'm gonna tear this cunt up, bitch. I love the taste of your pussy juice. Keep it coming." Between his mouth, fingers, and words, she screamed as she came. Her feet were planted wide and he sat back to watch his fingers shoving in and pulling out of her tunnel. "I could stay like this for hours, the problem with that is, my cock is so fucking hard that if I don't get it in now, you're going to be wearing my cum all over your belly." He moved in close, pulled her hips up, and shoved his cock deep.

Amy cried out again, he was so wide and stretched her vaginal tunnel to the point of pain. She wasn't nearly wet enough for the kind of fucking he was doing, but she held onto his shoulders and took his rough use of her body and she loved every minute of it. She came again as his cock spewed sperm deep inside at the mouth of her cervix. "Yes, give me all of it, every inch. I need. Damn it, oh yeah, just like that."

Baron was asleep before his cock softened enough to leave her body. She couldn't believe it. He screwed her like a maniac and then fell asleep with his head on her breast, while he was still in a crouched position over her. She tried to push him to the side, but he was too heavy for her to budge. The solution to pinch his nose did the trick. His eyes opened, and she told him to move. He began to pump his hips halfheartedly, and she shoved his shoulders. "No, you fool, I mean move off me, you're too damn heavy to sleep on top of me."

He nodded his head and began to lower it again until she grabbed a handful of his hair and shook his head a few times. "Get off me." His big body fell sideways off her and onto the bed next to her. He immediately rolled onto his back and began to snore. She giggled and went to the bathroom to clean up a bit, so she could be comfortable while she slept the rest of the night with him by her side.

*****

They planned to pick up Gunner from the hospital in the afternoon, but Amy wanted to stop off at the grocery store and buy a few more items to take home with them. She had been living with Baron for two weeks now and visiting Gunner every day. She found out that he had a terrible sweet tooth and loved her chocolate chunk oatmeal cookies. He liked Heavy Metal, and some Country music. She shared her life story with him and he sympathized with her grandparents.

She kept him entertained with Melvin stories and her observations of life at the clubhouse. "Myrtle finally allowed Gomer to move back into her place. He had to promise to clean the toilet when he was finished. He caved. You should have seen the look on her face when he told her he wouldn't expect her to clean up after his, and I am quoting Myrtle here, "filthy assed habits". He has to shower at least every other day, and if he isn't showered, he has to sleep in the basement. I think she loves him, but he has been on his own way too long. He is really catching hell from some of the guys, but he told Baron that they could rag on him all they want, he was the one taking Myrtle home, and he was the one sleeping in her bed." She fell silent and Gunner asked her outright.

"Baron's had you sleeping in his bed for the past two weeks, is it going to be a problem when I move in?"

It was the first time the subject had come up, and she wasn't about to tell him in the hospital that Baron missed having his friend to double team their lover, there were times he would have her wear a butt plug or a dildo strapped into place while he enjoyed filling her with his prick. Even with Gunner home it would be strange, but she loved the two of them. One without the other was all right, but both made her inner slut want to come out and play with them. She leaned over to whisper into his ear.

"Ever since you woke up and looked at me with those sexy eyes, and smiled at me, showing those dimples, my body has been waiting for you to come home." She squeaked when his hand grabbed the front of the shirt she was wearing and pulled her down to him so he could kiss her lips with promises of things to come.

She pushed the cart down the grocery aisle and ran into two of her former clients. They asked when she would be reopening her business, "Ninja is beginning to look like a ragamuffin, we have been waiting for you to open, but if you're not going to anytime soon, I will have to take her into Sheridan. I have to drive two hours for her to be groomed." The conversation depressed her. Ninja was a black toy poodle with a serious Fro hairdo. The little guy had won trophies and ribbons for the past three years, and his owner was understandably upset. She told Ninja's owner that she would call just as soon as she knew where she would be re-locating the shop.

Baron met her at the truck, and he hefted the bags into the bed under the canvas snap on cover. They went straight to the hospital and sprung Gunner, who was debating with a female nurse about leaving the hospital in a wheelchair. When he saw neither of them would step in and defend his position, he gave in grudgingly.

Amy read and re-read the discharge papers so she would know exactly what the doctors wanted Gunner to do. He was going to chafe at the no putting pressure on his leg, and she felt fortunate that he hadn't complained when she told him that Baron and some of the boys "built a ramp for you to drive your wheelchair up and down."

She'd helped Baron take the bed apart and place the mattress on top of the box springs on the floor so Gunner wouldn't be isolated in a hospital bed by himself. He had to take the left side of the bed to avoid having his leg and shoulder bumped during the night, so there was a tilt table for him to look through magazines or eat a meal in bed if he didn't feel like getting up. The TV remote was on the nightstand within easy reach, and she had set mason jars full of snacks on the table so he could satisfy his sweet tooth at will.

The first thing he wanted when they had him settled in his new motorized wheelchair was Amy. He'd driven to the dining room table and patted the shining wooden piece of furniture. "I want your ass right up here, legs spread and ready for me." She rushed into the bathroom and took a quick shower before complying with his demand. His obvious need fueled hers and while she was still damp from her shower, dampness of a different kind was starting to leak from the folds of her pussy.

She sat on the table and swung her leg over his head to brace her foot on the table's edge. He leaned in and inhaled her scent, closing his eyes and smiling when he caught the aroma of her arousal. His tongue slowly licked from the bottom of her slick slit, up to her clit. Her first orgasm was brought on with him tormenting her clit, the second was brought with his tongue and fingers. As she lay there gasping for breath, he backed his chair from the table and looked at her, "You taste as good as you look, but I need to know now, will you do what I tell you? Are you going to take what I dish out and be ready for more?

"I'm trying to use my brains here instead of my prick. If you're not planning to invest yourself in this relationship, say something now. I figured out a few things about myself while I've been lying in that damn bed. Life is too fuckin' short to try to change someone into what you want them to be. I'm looking for permanent. If you plan to leave, or only staying until I am healed, get the fuck out now. I don't need or want a pity fuck. If you are staying, then crawl over here and suck my cock. If not then Baron will have to make up his mind what he wants to do about you. I might love you, but I'll be damned if I'll be strung along hoping you will come to care half as much for me as I do for you."

Baron sat in the chair not saying a word. They'd already had this discussion last night, and she knew what was in his heart matched her feelings for him. Screaming, "I love you" at the top of her lungs, and whispering it again as she stared into his eyes after they'd made love. Well, that tended to be an icebreaker for just about any discussion.

She climbed down from the table and stood there, propping herself against it. She ignored her nudity and concentrated on what she wanted to say to this handsome asshole.

"If you wanted your cock sucked, all you had to do was ask. If you want a mindless whore, you are looking at the wrong woman, I can and will have an opinion. If we are making love, I love it when you two go all he-man Neanderthal on me, it makes me wet. I'm not built for the life of a fuck toy either. Not to mention, I like my spankings. If you get your head out of your ass long enough you'd remember how my body reacts to your hands.

"I plan to re-open my business because I'm not a user, and you two have work to do too. Baron and I talked last night about the three of us living and

162

loving together. I need to tell you that if you're just fucking with me, I swear I will do a lap dance on your damn grave. I happen to love you guys. Now unsnap your damn pants so I can get at your cock. If you haven't scared him off. Maybe Baron could find a way to fuck me while I'm busy with your prick." She went to her knees and began to crawl toward him, with her head up and a knowing smile on her lips.

The kiss of a leather strap on her ass made her pause for a second, she inhaled a deep breath and shivered. With each movement of her hips, she felt the kiss of leather stinging her ass cheeks and making them burn. When she got to Gunner, his thick cock was waiting for her and she used both hands to caress the hardened muscle encased in smooth satin. "May I?"

He nodded and she took the head of his cock, putting it to her pursed lips, slowly suctioning his flesh inside her warm wet mouth. He groaned, her eyes were looking up at his as he saw his cock disappear. He felt it when she adjusted her legs to spread them wide for Baron to enjoy at will. His hands fisted in her curls as he pushed her head further down. "That's right, suck my cock, I love this mouth of yours." Whatever Baron was doing at her other end must be making an impression, because the vibration of her moans went straight to his prick. Her mouth opened wider and his prick shoved deeper into the back of her throat as she screamed. He looked back to where Baron was and grinned when he saw that her little asshole was being stretched by Baron's wide cock, his hands were nowhere in sight, but Gunner would bet they were playing with her juicy cunt. He felt the way his balls tightened and knew he was about to squirt his cum down her throat.

"I'm getting ready to come, and you'd better be ready to swallow every fuckin' drop." Her strangled answer made no sense, but he tightened his hold on her hair and emptied his load into her throat. Feeling her swallowing increased his pleasure, and he yelled her name as the last drops were sucked out of his prick. He had to lift her head from his cock to get her to stop. He rubbed her shoulders as she gasped, and finally screamed in her own pleasure just as Baron slammed deep for the last bit of friction as his orgasm erupted.

Later that night, she rode Gunner while Baron watched and commented about how hot the show they were putting on was. "I swear, that is so fuckin' hot, seeing your cock slide inside that pussy." He came close and she saw the thick prick being offered to her. She opened her mouth and gave him what he needed.

*****

*Two Weeks Later...*

Baron and Gunner were enjoying a beer and shooting the shit with the guys at the clubhouse. It was getting late, but it was Friday night, so they could crash there if they needed to. The brothers were enjoying watching the slut's attentions, and a few of the club's Bitches strutted around in little or nothing outfits. The music was thumping and Baron looked around the room. He was completely content now. They had publicly claimed Amy, given her the tag Stretch, and presented her with a cut with both men's insignias on it.

The guys in the club loved her, especially since she had been making it a habit to cook dinners at the club on Friday nights. When the music stopped for a few minutes, and half of the lights in the room went out, Baron started to get up, intending to check the breaker panel.

Suddenly a bluesy thumping beat started up and Charm and Friendly were dancing on the miniscule stage. Peter Gabriel's "Sledgehammer" blared from the speakers as Stretch strutted from between the two women. She was wearing their cut and a few scraps of string, with nothing else but the five inch heels on her over the knee black leather boots. She grabbed the stripper pole and worked it like the pro she was, then strutted to the music's beat over to where her men sat.

She grinned at the looks they were sending her way. She knew she was cashing a check that her ass would be paying for later tonight, but that was part of the fun. She loved her life with her men.

# EPILOGUE

War was sick of the shit happening around him. He had been reluctant to take the "honor" when he'd been tapped as a bodyguard for the National President of Lucifer's Breed MC, and that reluctance had stayed with him ever since. Wolfgang had been leading the Breed for the past ten years, and when he caught wind that over half of the chapters were making it plain that they wanted new leadership, he visited the chapters, tapping their Presidents to be his guards. Without outright challenging the man, War couldn't refuse the invitation.

He'd been here for close to six months and was fed up with the backstabbing political shit. Wolf already had his personal Van Guard. He and four other former chapter presidents were just there as window dressing, a way for Wolf to keep a leash on the chapters they'd come from. He knew the same people that wanted Wolfman out would place him in the vacant seat, but until there was a new provable charge against the man, War couldn't challenge him.

Combat was nothing new to him, he'd been a Marine from the day he turned eighteen years old until his older brother died and his mother begged him to come home. She had gone so far as to write to the Senator from the district they lived in and begged them to make him leave the service. He knew she was terrified that she would lose her only remaining child, but it was fucking embarrassing to

166

have a General call him on the carpet for being selfish and causing his family so much anxiety that she'd written to the President of the United States, begging him to spare her only child's life.

It was ironic that he'd gotten home in time to be with her to watch her suffer through chemotherapy, and two operations for cancer, before dying later that year. She had been the last of her direct line and so had his father. She made him promise to marry and have children on her deathbed. So far, he hadn't found a female worth his time to lock down with, and right now he wasn't in a position to do the daddy gig either.

Ferdinand and King Ben had been found with foaming mouths, where somehow, they'd swallowed drain cleaner. Now two more men had been found in the same way. These last men were part of Wolfman's favorite inner circle of friends.

For a place that was the national mother charter club, it was a shithole. No one cleaned anything, and the old scarred tables and crates that were used as chairs kept their asses from being forced to sit on the filthy floor. It was originally a service station, and for the ten men that had started Lucifer's Breed, it was adequate. For a national headquarters, it showed a lack of pride and wealth.

There was a large basement where the druggies and whores slept, but that was it. There had been four rundown trailers towed into the back lot and some of the members called the places home. The bitches belonging to the club used the middle trailer for what little privacy they were allowed.

He'd found a building the club could pick up fairly cheap that would house a hundred people if they wanted to do some work on the old buildings. It was actually situated almost directly across the street from where they were now, setting behind the woods. The old winery had a big fuckin' cement block barn and the main building was block and rock construction. There would be plenty of room, seclusion, and the place was impressive to look at. The club didn't need expensive and Wall Street pretty, it needed presence.

There was only one other man that might sway some of the votes if he chose to declare himself a candidate for the Presidency, and War acknowledged that Race would be a good man for the job. Both of their fathers had been originals, except War's old man was killed ten years later by a rival gang. What happened to Race's father he didn't know or particularly cared to ask. Maybe they should talk, clear the growing animosity between them.

There was room for both men, providing one didn't mind taking a backseat, say Prez and Vice. He could live with that.

# ABOUT THE AUTHOR

## RYDER DANE

I write about MC Groups aka Biker Books, because I've lived with Motorcycles my entire life. It made me smile when a reviewing reader said that there was a realistic feel to my writing! Having been an "Old Lady" since I was 19 gives me the advantage of using a few real details of MC life. I am very happy to bring readers my stories and having them invest in my characters' lives.

Website: Ryderdane.com


Books by Ryder Dane
Big Dog (Burning Bastards MC Book 1)
Nomad's Fall (Burning Bastards MC Book 2)
Charlie's Heart
(Burning Bastards MC Series Book 3)

Sanctuary Within the Breed
(Lucifer's Breed MC Book 1)
Integrity Has No Bounds
(Lucifer's Breed MC Book 2)
Starting Over (Lucifer's Breed MC Book 3)